THE VANISHING GAME

HARDYBOYS ADVENTURES™

#3 *THE VANISHING GAME*

FRANKLIN W. DIXON

ALADDIN   New York London Toronto Sydney New Delhi

ALADDIN
An imprint of Simon & Schuster Children's Publishing Division
1230 Avenue of the Americas, New York, NY 10020
First Aladdin hardcover edition June 2013
Copyright © 2013 by Simon & Schuster, Inc.
All rights reserved, including the right of reproduction in whole or in part in any form.
ALADDIN is a trademark of Simon & Schuster, Inc.,
and related logo is a registered trademark of Simon & Schuster, Inc.
THE HARDY BOYS MYSTERY STORIES, HARDY BOYS ADVENTURES,
and related logo are trademarks of Simon & Schuster, Inc.
For information about special discounts for bulk purchases, please contact Simon & Schuster
Special Sales at 1-866-506-1949 or business@simonandschuster.com.
The Simon & Schuster Speakers Bureau can bring authors to your live event.
For more information or to book an event contact the Simon & Schuster Speakers Bureau
at 1-866-248-3049 or visit our website at www.simonspeakers.com.
The text of this book was set in Adobe Caslon Pro.
Manufactured in the United States of America 0513 FFG
2 4 6 8 10 9 7 5 3 1
Library of Congress Control Number 2013934005
ISBN 978-1-4424-7344-7 (hc)
ISBN 978-1-4424-5981-6 (pbk)
ISBN 978-1-4424-5982-3 (eBook)

CONTENTS

G-FORCED

1

FRANK

DID YOU KNOW THAT COTTON CANDY depends heavily on the molecular construction of sugar?" I asked brightly, grabbing a hunk of my brother Joe's fluffy pink confection and popping it into my mouth. "The cotton candy machine uses centrifugal force to spin hot sugar so quickly and cool it so rapidly, the sugar doesn't have time to recrystallize!"

My date—or so I'd been told, because she didn't seem super attached to me—Penelope Chung, rolled her eyes. "That's fascinating, Frank," she said, shooting a glare at her best friend, Daisy Rodriguez, who was Joe's date and the glue barely holding our foursome together. "Please tell me more about molecules. Or force times acceleration. Or the atomic properties of *fun*."

1

Joe coughed loudly, grabbing my shoulder and pulling me close enough to hear him mutter, "Ixnay on the ience-scay."

I couldn't help it. Joe is always telling me science isn't romantic, but *come on*. Isn't "romance" itself a scientific concept? Attraction, biology, all that stuff?

Daisy smiled, a little too enthusiastically. "Shall we head over to the G-Force?" she asked, looking hopefully from Penelope and me to Joe. "My dad said the first ride would be at eight o'clock. And it's just about quarter of."

"Yes!" Penelope cried before Joe or I could respond, grabbing Daisy's arm and pulling her ahead of us toward Funspot's new ride, G-Force. Penelope leaned close to Daisy's ear, and while I couldn't hear what she was saying, her tone did not sound warm.

Joe met my eye and sighed.

"I don't think she likes me," I told him.

Joe just shook his head and patted my back. "I think your powers of detection are dead-on true."

We started walking. "Sorry," I said. "I know you're really into Daisy."

Joe nodded. "It's okay, man," he said, holding out his cotton candy for me to take another hunk. "I just don't think you're Penelope's type."

I nodded. "But it's pretty cool that we get to be some of the first people to check out G-Force, right?"

"*Very* cool," Joe agreed.

G-Force was the new, premiere attraction at Funspot,

a small amusement park that had been a staple of Bayport summers for generations, but had been getting more and more run-down over the years. Last fall, Daisy's dad, Hector, had used their entire family's savings to buy the park from its longtime owner, Doug Spencer, who had fallen on hard times. Hector wanted to build Funspot into a top-tier amusement park—the kind of place people would drive hours to visit. His first step toward making that happen had been to install G-Force.

The ride was a new creation of Greg and Derek Piperato, better known as the Piperato Brothers—*the* hip new architects of premiere amusement rides all over the world. They built the HoverCoaster for Holiday Gardens in Copenhagen, the Loop-de-Loco for Ciudad de Jugar in Barcelona, and the ChillTaser for Bingo Village in Orlando, right here in the USA. These guys are seriously awesome at what they do. They know their physics, they know their architecture, and they keep coming up with new ideas to revolutionize the amusement industry.

They don't work cheap, though. According to Daisy, Hector had to take out a major loan to afford G-Force. And unfortunately, right after Hector signed the contracts— Funspot had exclusive rights to the ride for five years— Daisy's mom had been laid off from her job as a manager at some big bank in New York City. If Daisy and her family had hoped Funspot would be successful before, now their whole future was riding on the park's success.

"Wow," Joe breathed as we turned a corner, and there it was: G-Force!

For weeks, Hector had paid for advertisements on all the local radio stations: "Come to Funspot to ride G-Force! What does it do? You'll have to ride it to find out . . . but one thing's for sure"—here the voice got deep and creepy—*"you'll never be the same!"*

I had been sure that seeing the attraction would be a disappointment. I mean, how could you live up to that ad? Put aside the basic scientific impossibilities of its promises (*Never be the same?* What, would it change your molecular structure?); it was hard to imagine a ride so impressive that it could stand up to weeks of wondering what it might look like. But the structure in front of me was, in a word, *awesome*. It was sleek and silver and had the curved, aerodynamic shape of a spaceship.

"Wow," I echoed pointing at it like a kindergartner. "That thing is cool!"

Joe looked confused, then followed my gaze and nodded. "Oh, sure. It does look cool. But I was talking about the crowd—check it out!"

I looked around. Joe was right. The line coiled around several times before stretching all the way from the ride, through the "kiddie park" (where Joe and I had spent countless hours on the helicopter ride as kids), down the row of food stands, and nearly to the parking lot. When we'd arrived at the park hours earlier, it hadn't been nearly as long. But it looked like all those radio advertisements worked!

"Looks like a lot of people want to be g-forced!" I said, smiling, as Daisy and Penelope slowed their pace and we caught up to them.

Daisy looked thrilled. "I guess so!" she said, looking around at the crowd like she couldn't believe it. "It looks like the whole student body of Bayport High is here!"

Joe nodded, surveying the huge line. "We—uh—don't have to wait in that, do we?"

"Of course not." Daisy smiled and shook her head, gallantly taking Joe by the arm. "Follow me, mister. The four of us are skipping this line. It pays to have friends in high places!"

Penelope glanced at me warily, but we both fell into step behind Joe and Daisy. She'd been right: The line was crowded with our classmates from Bayport High. Some smiled and waved at Daisy as we passed, or called out their congratulations. But as we walked by one sullen-looking group of boys, a dark-haired kid stepped out and blocked Daisy's path.

"Well, well, well," he said, giving the four of us a not-very-friendly once-over. "What have we here? The kings and queens of Funspot?"

As Joe shot her a questioning glance, Daisy frowned at the kid. "Let us by, Luke."

He didn't move, but met her gaze without a smile. "Is this your new *boyfriend*?" He scowled at Joe.

Joe stepped forward, holding out his hand. "Hey, man . . ."

But Daisy just shook her head. "What do you care?" she asked, looking from the boy to his chuckling friends in line. "Joe, Frank, this is my *ex*-boyfriend, Luke."

"Emphasis on *ex*," Penelope piped up, stepping forward to give Luke a withering stare.

Luke glared at Penelope for a moment, but her words seemed to wound him, and he quickly looked down before stepping aside. Daisy hesitated for a moment, then turned around and walked briskly past. Penelope followed, her head held high, and Joe and I and began to follow.

"Hey!" Luke called after us when we were a few feet away, and Daisy was almost at the ride. "Congrats on the turnout tonight!"

Daisy paused, turning slowly to look back at him.

Luke's expression turned to an ugly smirk. "Guess you can go to college after all!" he shouted, loud enough for the crowd to hear. His group of friends erupted into loud chuckles. Daisy cringed.

Joe was furious. I could tell he was upset on Daisy's behalf and would have loved to teach Luke a lesson. But instead he pulled out his smartphone. "Smile," he said to Luke, snapping a picture.

Luke was taken aback. "What did you do that for?" he demanded angrily.

Joe just smiled. "When we go to security and tell them a

group is being rowdy and disruptive, this way they'll know who to look for."

Luke glared at Joe. I had to smile. I seriously doubted Joe had any intention of going to security—but the look on Luke's face made it clear he didn't know that.

Joe touched Daisy's arm. "Shall we?" he asked, gesturing to the ride.

Daisy looked like she wasn't sure what to do. Penelope shot Luke another icy look, then moved toward Daisy. "Let's go, Daze," she said, pushing her forward. "He's such a jerk."

After a moment, Daisy moved on, and the three of us followed close behind.

At the head of the line, an older, gruff-looking guy with ruddy skin and dark hair and beard stood behind a narrow metal gate. He looked at Daisy and nodded. "Miss." Without another word, he opened the gate, and the four of us walked through.

"Thanks, Cal," Daisy said, smiling brightly. "Do I have time to quickly show my friends the ride before it starts?"

Cal nodded, not making eye contact. He locked the gate, then led the four of us up a metal gangplank toward the shining, brushed-chrome ride. A small rectangular door was embedded in the side, and Cal easily pulled it open, gesturing for us to enter. Behind us, people were hooting and hollering, clearly eager to get onto the ride themselves.

Inside, small purple lights recessed into the ceiling and walls provided just enough light to make out a circle of huge, cushy seats, each with a sturdy restraining bar, surrounding an open center. I strained to see the ceiling, the floor, anything that would give a hint to what the ride actually *did*—but it was too dark.

"So . . . what does it do?" I asked Cal, who had paused in front of a bank of seats.

He turned to me and smiled. In the low purple light I could just make out that he was missing several teeth. He laughed, a low, raspy sound.

"I guess you'll just have to ride it and find out, won't you?" he asked. Then he nodded at the door. "Let's get you strapped in."

Daisy and Penelope smiled and eagerly chose seats next to each other. As Cal was securing the restraints around each of them, I glanced at my brother. I thought he looked pale.

"Are you okay?" I whispered. His eyes were darting around the ride nervously.

He bit his lip. "What do you think the ads meant," he whispered, "when they said, 'You'll never be the same'?"

I opened my mouth to answer, but Joe immediately held up his hand to shush me. "Never mind," he whispered. "I don't want Daisy to hear."

At that moment, Cal finished strapping in Penelope and looked back at us. Joe smiled eagerly—I mean, I guess it was supposed to look eager, but to me it looked kind of insane—and walked over to the seat next to Daisy. As he got strapped in, I settled into the seat next to Penelope.

She looked at me warily. "Great," she said tonelessly, "we get to ride together."

I nodded. "There was a rumor on amusementgeeks.com that this ride will send you into another dimension," I told her, "but of course that's scientifically impossible."

"Good to know," she said, and turned back to Daisy.

Cal came over and quickly strapped me in, placing two restraining belts over my shoulders and clicking a wide metal bar into place just inches from my stomach. He jiggled the bar a little to make sure it was tight, then, apparently satisfied, turned and exited the ride without a word.

"So, have you test-driven the ride?" Joe asked Daisy, breaking the silence.

She shook her head. "I wish," she said with a sigh. "But my dad's agreement with the Piperato Brothers was very specific. *No one*—except the test subjects they used when they were designing the ride, I guess—gets to ride G-Force before its official opening." She checked her watch. "Which happens—wow—in about three minutes!"

Before any of us could reply, the door opened again, and eager riders from the line began filing in, oohing and aahing, straining to get a good look at the ride's interior. They milled around and selected seats, and after a minute or so, Cal entered and began to strap all the riders in.

"So, Daisy," Brian Mullin, one of the football players,

spoke up. "Is this ride going to change my life, or what?"

Daisy chuckled. "You know what the ads say, Brian," she replied, deepening her voice. *"You'll never be the same."*

Brian snickered. "Well, I hope I come out taller."

Cal was just finishing strapping in the last rider, and as we all laughed at Brian's joke, he glanced around at all of us, then nodded. "Enjoy the ride," he said, not smiling, and then exited through the tiny door. It closed behind him, and the inside of the ride darkened even further.

Everyone grew quiet as we waited for the ride to begin. In the quiet, I picked up a weird clicking sound—like someone tapping their fingernails against a hard surface. I looked to my right, where the sound was coming from. Penelope was looking around too, seeming to hear it, and Daisy glanced at her and frowned, then turned to Joe.

"Are your *teeth chattering?*" she asked.

But Joe didn't get a chance to answer—at that very moment, the purple lights clicked off and we were immersed in darkness. A huge *whoosh* emanated from the floor—probably the ride's engine cranking up. Then a loud guitar chord sounded: I recognized it as the beginning of "Beautiful," a rock song that was climbing the charts. The song started up, and then suddenly we were moving—suddenly we were moving *really fast*! The circle of seats orbited faster and faster around the center, and I could feel the centrifugal force pushing me against the back of the seat. My head slammed back into the headrest, and it felt like the skin of my face was tightening, being pulled back by the force of the revolutions.

People began screaming, and suddenly the darkness was cut by a bright white light. I could make out the riders on the other side of the circle grimacing and beaming, screaming in fear and pleasure. Then the light cut out, then on again—a strobe light, making the whole ride look like it was in stop-motion.

The ride seemed to slow, and then suddenly the seats rose into the air. I gasped, exhilarated by the sudden motion. Just as quickly as they'd risen, though, they plunged down, farther, I think, than we'd been when the ride started. The strobe lights changed, suddenly, so that instead of bright white light, we saw neon images projected on the riders across from us symbols, photographs of beautiful nature scenes, crying babies, an old woman smiling. The ride kept spinning, ascending, descending, but as hard as I tried, I couldn't keep track of all its motions. The scientist in me had wanted to break down exactly what G-Force did, but in the end, I just couldn't. The experience of the ride took over, and I screamed and laughed with everyone else, feeling totally exhilarated.

After some time—it could have been seconds or it could have been hours—the ride spun around again, gluing us all back in our seats. I closed my eyes as the revolutions slowed, and the music began to fade. Slower, slower, slower still we circled, until finally I felt the ride click into its resting position. I opened my eyes as the purple lights kicked on again, illuminating the ride with dim light.

Everyone looked like they'd been tumble dried. Hair stuck out in all directions, clothes were rumpled, expressions dazed. But as we all looked at one another, not sure how to capture the experience, suddenly Brian Mullin began to clap slowly. The girl on his right joined in, and after a few seconds, so did everyone else on the ride.

"That was AWESOME!" Brian shouted.

His words seemed to give everyone else permission to speak too.

"That was AMAZING. . . ."

". . . unreal . . ."

"I've never felt anything like that."

"Omigosh, I want to ride that, like, *ten* more times!"

I looked over at Daisy, who looked a little dazed herself, but a smile was creeping slowly to her lips. Joe (who looked less pale now) smiled at her and took her hand, giving it a little squeeze.

"Looks like Funspot's new main attraction is a hit," I heard him whisper to her.

But as everyone seemed to be giving their personal review of the ride, an increasingly concerned voice broke through the din.

"Kelly?"

Penelope sat up, grinning, and patted Daisy's shoulder. "Good job, Hector," she said. "I think he bought a winner!"

"Kelly?"

I looked across the ride, where the voice was coming from. People were gradually stopping their own conversations, turning their attention to the spot where a girl about our age struggled against the restraints, stretching her neck to look around.

"Kelly? KELLY!"

The girl let out a sob.

"Oh no!" she cried. "No, no, no! Where is she?"

That's when I caught sight of the seat next to her.

"My sister *disappeared*!"

It was empty. And the restraints that should have held Kelly in place had been cut.

THE DEATH RIDE

2

JOE

"COMING UP AT NOON," THE SMALL television on our kitchen counter blared, "the owner of Funspot responds to allegations that his newest attraction is a *death ride*." The image cut to grainy footage of Hector Rodriguez walking to his car in the Funspot parking lot, trailed by a crew of reporters and cameramen.

"Mr. Rodriguez," one woman trilled, shoving a microphone at him, "did you know G-Force was this dangerous?"

Across the table, Frank groaned. "She's not *dead*," he said with a sigh; "she's *missing*."

"Missing with no trace," I added, pushing my eggs around my plate. It was the following Friday, six days since Kelly Keohane went missing, and somehow, whenever the incident

14

was mentioned, I lost my appetite. "No footprints, no finger-prints, no cell phone records, no witnesses reporting any sign of her." I sighed. "It's like she just disappeared into thin air!"

Frank nodded and shot me a concerned look. "Have you talked to Daisy?"

I frowned. "I keep trying," I replied, shrugging. "She doesn't return my calls. I talked to her really quick between classes yesterday, and she said she's not mad at me—just stressed out."

"They must have a lot on their minds," Frank agreed.

I could imagine. Funspot had been the talk of the town since G-Force opened—and not in a good way. I was sure Daisy's father was regretting his decision to invest in the new, expensive ride.

Frank stood and clapped me on the back. "Come on," he said, grabbing his book bag. "Let's get going. Maybe we'll find something new out at school."

I put down my fork and got my stuff together without answering. I knew Frank was trying to be positive, but any news we'd gotten about Funspot hadn't been good.

"Aaaaaanyway," Jamie King was saying, flicking a high-lighted blond lock behind her shoulder with a long purple fingernail, "I was like, 'Are you serious?' I mean, do you really think I'd ever go out with you?"

She smiled at all of us who surrounded her at a lunch table. Daisy had grabbed me after history class and apologized for being so distant lately; she'd invited Frank and me to sit with her friends at lunch. So far, sitting at a girls' lunch table was not so exciting.

"You know?" Jamie went on, looking around at her girlfriends, not satisfied with their reaction. "Daisy? Am I right?"

Daisy didn't respond. She was staring into her vegetarian chili like it held the secrets of the universe. I didn't think she'd even heard Jamie.

I was sitting next to her, so I gave her a nudge. "Daisy? You okay?"

She looked up, startled. "Sorry—did you say something, Joe?"

"No, but *I* did," Jamie said, pointing to herself. "I was talking about this guy who came up to me while I was working at Funspot last night. I swear, people just love entertainers."

Over lunch, Frank and I had learned that Daisy had gotten Jamie a job singing and dancing in the Funspot Revue at the park. They had wanted her to wear a big Fannie the Funspot Falcon costume, but she convinced them to let her be Princess Funfara instead.

Daisy sighed. "I guess we should be happy that there was even anybody *in* the park to approach you," she said, poking her chili with a spoon. "Attendance has been down ever since the G-Force opening. *Way* down."

Penelope, who was sitting across from us next to Frank, shot Daisy a look of concern. "When can you open it again?" she asked.

"Tonight," Daisy said without excitement, "but I can't imagine that many people are going to show up to go on a ride that was involved in a girl's disappearance. The inspectors didn't find anything wrong with it, but everyone's still calling G-Force 'the Death Ride.'" She spooned a bite of chili into her mouth, then grimaced.

Jamie looked thoughtful. "I bet that girl ran off on her own," she said, pointing a carrot stick at us. "She could have had trouble at home. You don't know."

Daisy just shook her head.

Jamie bit into her carrot stick with a loud *crunch* and chewed. "What you need," she said after a minute, "is someone to look into it. Someone besides the police." She looked up at Frank and me. "Someone like these two!"

Penelope looked at her like she was nuts. "These two?"

Jamie nodded, giving me a frankly appraising look. "They investigate things for people. You didn't know that?"

Frank blushed and coughed on his tuna sandwich.

Jamie chomped on another carrot stick and turned away with a mysterious expression.

I was beginning to think Jamie knew everything about everybody at Bayport High.

Daisy seemed to be coming out of her fog a little bit. She looked at me thoughtfully. "*Would* you guys look into it for us?" she asked. "I know you're both smart. We could really use someone to help us get to the bottom of this. I don't know what we could pay you, but . . ."

Frank waved his hand dismissively. "We don't need any money," he said. "We just help out friends."

Daisy smiled. It was the first time since G-Force opened that I'd seen anything like hope on her face. "Am I a friend?" she asked.

"You," I said, putting my hand on her shoulder, "are such a good friend, we'll get started on this today."

Julie Keohane was in gym class with me. In fact, she had once knocked me to the ground in a particularly heated basketball game. She was Kelly's sister—now the missing Kelly. A crowd of students surrounded her after our daily run to give her their condolences. After gym class today—a particularly embarrassing lesson called Dances of the World—I ran up to Julie to offer my sympathies and see if I could ask her a few questions.

We sat on a bench outside the locker rooms. "Are you and Kelly close?" I asked gently.

Julie nodded. "Very close," she said, and sniffled. "She's fourteen, only two years younger than me. We tell each other everything."

I nodded. "Has anything been going on with Kelly that's out of the ordinary?" I asked. "A new boyfriend, or an argument with someone?"

Julie looked up from the spot on the ground she'd been staring at. "No," she said, a little forcefully.

Hmm. "Does Kelly get along well with your parents?" I asked. "Do you guys ever fight?"

Julie sighed. "She gets along with everyone," she said, sounding exasperated. "Look, I know where you're going with this. I know you want me to say someone was mad at her, so you can tell the police or whoever that she ran away or something."

I paused. "I wasn't trying to get you to say that," I said, although I'd kind of been hoping she would. I really wanted to find out what had happened to Kelly. If she could give me a reason Kelly might have run away, at least that would make sense. Right now nothing about this made sense. "I just want you to tell me the truth, so I can help figure out what happened to her."

Julie widened her eyes. "She *disappeared* on that *ride*," she said, then shrugged in frustration. "I don't get it either. I know it's weird. But when the ride started, she was strapped in right next to me, and I could hear her screaming with everyone else. When the ride was over, I looked and she was gone. The restraints were cut. She didn't *run away*. She didn't go with someone. Kelly was a good kid. She always told me or my parents what she was doing."

She stood, then stopped and leaned down, saying these next words right into my face. "*Someone took her*," she hissed. "And that scares me more than anything."

I was a little shaken by my conversation with Julie, so I didn't try to talk to anyone else for the next two periods until school ended. When I went outside to meet Frank at our usual meeting spot, though, I saw him talking to a group of boys who had been waiting to ride G-Force that night.

"It was a guy I'd never seen before," one of them was saying. "He got *out* of line, which I thought was weird."

"He was pretty close to the front, too," one of the other guys said.

"Yeah," said the first guy. "And I saw him on one side of the ride, then the other, like he was circling it."

Frank glanced at me and nodded. "Thanks, guys. Joe, this is Dave and Eli. Guys, this is my brother, Joe. What did the guy look like again?"

The first guy, Dave, didn't hesitate. "He had dark hair and blue eyes, and he had freckles. He was about this tall." He gestured a few inches above his own head.

That description sounded very familiar. Unpleasantly familiar. It suited Daisy's ex-boyfriend, Luke Costigan, to a T. I took out my phone and showed them the picture I had taken of Luke. They nodded—that was Luke, all right.

Frank thanked the boys and sent them on their way as I mulled this over. Finally he turned to me.

"Sounds like Luke, right?"

I nodded. "The one and only."

Frank looked thoughtful. "We know he's a jerk," he said. "Is he enough of a jerk to sabotage a ride opening to get back at Daisy for breaking his heart?"

ARE YOU READY?

3

FRANK

THE NEXT MORNING WAS A SATURDAY, but no sleeping in for Joe or me. No, we were up at the crack of dawn to get to Funspot before it opened. The security guard told us that Daisy had warned him we were coming, and ushered us into the employee entrance. As elephants, giraffes, and pirates struggled to get their huge stuffed heads situated *just right*, a mustached man who had to be Hector Rodriguez walked up to us and held out his hand.

"You must be the Hardy Boys," he said, offering a megawatt smile that showed off a row of perfect white teeth. "Thank you so much for looking into this for my family. We are very grateful."

Joe held up a finger. "We're happy to help out our friends.

But if you could keep the fact that we're doing this under your hat . . ."

"Yes," I chimed in. "We've found that working undercover makes it easier to look around and get information."

Hector looked from my brother to me. "Of course. I won't tell anyone you're working here, if that's what you mean."

"Excellent," I said. "Okay, can you show us the ride?"

Hector nodded and turned to lead us out of the employees-only area, through the food stalls, and past the kiddie park. And then there it was, in front of us: G-Force, the sleek, enigmatic ride that had blown me away.

I assumed the park was still pretty empty, so I started when I saw someone moving in the glass-paneled control booth that jutted out from the side. On further inspection, I realized that it was Cal, the ride operator from the week before. He opened the door to the booth and shuffled down the steps, not making eye contact.

"I know you boys both were on the ride on Saturday night, so you know the basics," Hector said.

"We did," I agreed, "and it really is an amazing ride, Mr. Rodriguez."

He shook his head. "Please, call me Hector," he said. "And thank you. I really thought we had a winner here . . . until, well, all this happened."

Joe nodded sympathetically. "Hector, do you have any

idea what happened to the girl?" he asked. "Any idea at all?"

Hector sighed and shook his head. "I'm as stumped as everyone else," he replied. "We searched the ride, the whole park. Nobody has seen anybody matching Kelly's description in a twenty-mile radius. It's like she just vanished."

He stopped, sighing again and looking down at the ground, then raised his eyes to meet Cal's. "Boys, this is Cal Nevins," he said, "G-Force's first and only ride operator. I'd bet he knows this ride almost as well as the brothers who designed it. He can take you inside and answer any questions you have."

"Great, thanks," I said, nodding at Cal. He nodded back at me, making eye contact for only a second, and then turned back toward the ride.

"Should we go in?" he asked.

Joe caught my eye. I could tell from the tiny bit of fear in his eyes—invisible to anybody except his brother, I'm sure—that he wasn't exactly looking forward to riding this thing again.

"We should," I said. "And hopefully we'll find something that will tell us what happened to Kelly."

"So how does it work, exactly?" Joe asked for what seemed like the hundredth time, running his hand along the sleek silver walls of the inside of G-Force.

"I keep telling you," Cal replied gruffly—and accurately, "it's a mixture of a few things. Shifting perspective, strobe lights, and centrifugal force." He sounded as though he were quoting directly from the ride's manual.

"And there's absolutely nowhere for anyone to hide in here?" I asked, looking around the ride with a careful eye. Cal had turned on all the interior lights, making it much brighter than it had been on the night of its opening. But I still couldn't find anything suspicious. Inside, the ride was just as sleek as it was outside, with brushed silver metal forming the sharply curved walls. Aside from the main door, there didn't seem to be any way to get in or out, or anywhere to stay out of sight.

Cal sighed. "Not that I'm aware of." He paused, looking around the ride with a faraway expression. "I've racked my brain trying to figure out what happened to that poor girl," he added. "But I've got nothin'."

I nodded, frowning. "I think," I said, "we're just going to have to ride it again."

Joe paled a little. But he seemed to push past his fear as he sat down in one of the cushy purple seats and put his game face on.

"Let's do this," he said, clutching the restraint bar. "For Kelly!"

Cal strapped us both in and walked out to the control booth, shutting the door behind him. The lights went down, then out entirely. I heard the same *whoosh* sound as we had the previous Saturday.

"Joe?" I asked as the first guitar chord of "Beautiful" played, because his silence was starting to freak me out.

"Frank, was this a mistake?" Joe asked, but before I could answer him, the music crescendoed and the strobe lights started up and we started moving, and pretty soon I couldn't think about anything but how awesome this ride was. Every so often I would catch myself and try to focus: *Look around! Observe! Listen for strange noises! Check the strength of my harness!* But I could barely see anything through the flashing lights, fog, and random images. I couldn't even see Joe anymore.

Wait.

"Joe?" I yelled.

No answer. The music wailed, a flower wilted, a sad-looking toddler pointed her finger at me accusingly. Then the strobe lights started up again.

"JOE?"

The ride started slowing down. I could feel the seats returning to their original orbit, and the music was quieting, reaching the end of the song. I blinked, shaking my head and trying to squint through the darkness for my brother. He'd been right across from me . . . right? Or was he next to me? Or . . .

The images faded and the lights cut out. We were

plunged into darkness. I closed my eyes and reached up to touch my head, almost wondering if it was still there. My brain felt like it was bouncing around in my skull, after being flung this way and that for however long the ride lasted (I honestly had no idea).

"Joe?" I asked again, rubbing my temples and opening my eyes. The weak purple lights flickered back on.

Joe sat across from me, looking like he'd just stumbled in from a hurricane. His straw-colored hair poked out in random directions. His clothes were mussed. He looked like he was sweating.

He blinked and looked over at me. "Yeah?"

I glared at him. "Why didn't you *answer* me during the *ride*?"

He blinked again. "You said something?"

Before I could reply, the small door was pushed open, letting in a ray of sunlight, and the dark profile of Cal appeared. "You boys see anything suspicious?" he asked curiously.

I sighed.

"No," I said. "I think we're going to have to ride it again."

And again. And again.

Joe looked awful. After the fifth ride, he asked Cal to unharness him, stood up, ran out of the ride, and returned a few minutes later.

"All right," he said, settling back into his seat. "Strap me in and fire this baby up again."

Cal looked impressed despite himself. "Okay." He did

as Joe asked, then walked out of the ride, closing the door behind him.

"Joe," I said, "are you okay?"

Joe coughed. "I am not okay," he replied, "but at least Aunt Trudy didn't make us a huge breakfast today."

I groaned. My own head was pounding, and the ride was beginning to hurt, not feel awesome.

"Maybe we should take a break," I suggested. "This is going nowhere. We're five rides in and I still haven't noticed anything that might explain what happened to Kelly. Have you?"

Joe winced and shook his head. "I have noticed the contents of my stomach," he replied. "That's it."

I tried to sit up. "Those boys I talked to yesterday—they said they saw Luke getting out of line. Remember?"

"And he circled the ride," Joe added, life coming back to his eyes.

"Maybe we could get out and walk around the ride?" I suggested. "See if we notice anything unusual?"

Joe nodded. "Yes. Yes, please!"

I looked at my brother. We both seemed to reach the same realization at the same time.

"CAL!!!" we screamed.

But it was too late. The lights went off, and the *whoosh* of the motor started up again.

I would say that our last, unnecessary ride on G-Force that morning wasn't so bad, but really? It was. Joe barfed again afterward. I was pretty sure my brain had become permanently unstuck from my skull and would just rattle around in there for the rest of my life.

But the good news? I don't think I had ever appreciated solid ground as much as I did when we got off the ride. I walked around, stamping my feet into the ground, enjoying the pleasant, solid resistance. It was like slipping between the sheets of the world's most comfortable bed after sleeping on the floor for a week.

"You see anything?" Cal asked, following Joe and me down onto the ground. "In the ride, I mean? Did it help?"

"We didn't see anything, but it did help," I told him. "I guess we just need to think about it a little more. In the meantime, we're going to look around outside. Is that okay?"

Cal looked surprised, but he quickly nodded. "Sure. Sure, whatever you think will help."

He backed off, and Joe and I took another minute or two for the world to stop spinning before we walked over to the smooth metal side of G-Force. Apart from the one entrance, there were no hinges or doors; not even a seam so you could clearly see where the sheets of metal had been hammered together. It simply looked like it had dropped out of the sky, sleek, shiny, and fully formed.

"See anything?" I asked Joe after a minute or two.

"No," he said with a sigh, "but let's take our time here. Maybe Luke dropped something in the grass. Or maybe we'll spot something of Kelly's."

I agreed, and we slowed our progress, making sure to take in everything we possibly could. It was about half an hour before we reached its far side, and the ride cut us off from the early-morning sun, plunging us in shadow.

I was running my hand along the ride's outer surface when I heard a nightmarish cackle behind me, followed by a creepy voice:

"Are you ready to ride . . . THE DEATH RIDE?"

PUBLIC RELATIONS

4

JOE

JUMPED ABOUT TEN FEET IN THE AIR. OR THAT'S how it felt. I'm not ashamed. You have to remember that I was in a delicate state, with my brains all scrambled into a gray-matter omelet, and that I had recently vomited not once, but twice. Truly, I was operating on a nutritional loss. Plus, that voice was just *creepy*.

So imagine how foolish I felt when I turned around and saw not the terrifying bat-demon of my nightmares (I mean, some of them), but two hipsterish dudes, wearing matching fedoras and laughing hysterically.

"We got you!" one of them, a redhead, yelled, pointing at us.

"You got us, all right," Frank replied, deadpan, straightening up. "You sure got us!"

I should mention here that, once the shock wore off

and I was able to be more observant, it became apparent that both of these guys were dressed like gangsters from the 1920s or something. Fedoras, striped trousers, vests, oxfords, funny little bow ties, the works. And they each had mustaches that had been waxed—yeah, waxed—into different shapes.

"Who are you?" I asked, seriously curious now.

The redhead was still too busy cackling to reply. But his friend, a blond with sausage curls, stood up straight and then gave me a formal bow. "Pleased to meet you, good sir," he said. "*We* . . . are the Piperato Brothers!"

"*The* Piperato Brothers?" Frank asked, his jaw suddenly on the ground. "The guys who designed G-Force—and, like, a million other rides?"

Frank never says "like," so I figured I was on my own as far as getting useful information out of these weirdos.

"I'm Joe Hardy, and this is my brother, Frank," I said. Then I asked, "What are you two doing here? We heard you were at the opening of a HoverCoaster in New Zealand or something."

"Correction," said the redhead, holding up a finger, "we *were* at the opening of the PhantomRider in Christchurch. But at about seven o'clock last night, we arrived at the airport."

Frank seemed to be returning to earth. "Did you come because of the disappearance?" he asked.

The blond one cut his eyes at Frank. "If you mean the

incident last Saturday night, then yes, that is why we're here." He straightened up and suddenly put on a serious face. "When something like this happens, you only get a brief window to add your spin to the story. That's what Greg and I are here to do."

I raised my eyebrows. "You have a theory about what happened to Kelly?" I asked.

The redhead—Greg, I guessed—shook his head. "Not exactly," he said. "But Derek and I do have theories about how to handle the press."

I glanced at Frank. Hmm. "It sounds like you guys need to talk to Hector," I said. "You know, the owner of Funspot?"

Derek nodded, pulling the latest iPhone out of his pocket and jabbing at it with his narrow fingers. "That's right," he said, squinting at the screen. "One . . . Hector Rodriguez. Would you know where we can find him?"

"Sure," I said, shooting a quick *Go along with me* look at my brother. I had the feeling we were going to want to hear what these guys had to say. "We can take you back to his office. I'm sure he'll be there."

We started walking back toward the entrance we'd come in that morning, where the administration building stood. I knew from Daisy that Hector's office was inside on the second floor. As we walked, Frank peppered the brothers with questions about their most recent roller coasters and thrill rides, and the brothers seemed to lap up his attention like two cats licking up cream.

Back at the administration building, employees were gathering in the lobby, fixing up their character costumes and strapping on their change belts. It was almost time for the park to open, and the place was starting to buzz with activity. A quick glance at the parking lot confirmed my fears: There didn't seem to be any customers waiting to get in. It was another reminder that Frank and I needed to get to the bottom of this—for Daisy.

"Hector's office is in here," I said, leading the Piperato Brothers through the glass doors of the administration building.

"You've really never been here before?" Frank asked the brothers as we led everyone up a flight of stairs.

"Indeed no," Greg replied. "Actually, it's rare that we get a chance to come out to a park and see our rides in action."

"But you said you just got in from doing that in New Zealand," I pointed out.

Derek chuckled. "Yeah, but that was *New Zealand*," he said. "The park owners were nice enough to pay for our flights and hotel. No offense, but Baytown just doesn't hold the same appeal."

I raised an eyebrow. "It's Bay*port*," I said.

"What Derek means," Greg cut in, with a conciliatory smile (I was getting that Greg was perhaps the nicer of the two), "is that we're usually very busy in our lab designing the rides of the future. Sadly, we just don't get a lot of time to travel."

We were outside Hector's office now, so I just smiled

and knocked on the door before we entered "How lucky for us to get to meet you."

Inside, the office wasn't glamorous. Faux wood paneling that looked at least thirty years old covered the walls, and wrinkled, framed maps of Funspot during different times in its history were the only decoration. The office was really a glorified closet—there was barely room for Frank, the Piperato Brothers, and me to stand facing Hector's old wooden desk.

Hector looked surprised. "Hello?" he asked, looking from me to Frank. Then his eyes settled on the fedora'ed faces of the duo who'd been expected to save Funspot. "It can't be . . . Derek and Greg Piperato?" He stood.

"None other, good sir," Derek replied, firing out a hand for Hector to shake. Hector did, slowly, staring at the brothers like they were some kind of apparition. "And you must be Mr. Rodriguez, the forward-thinking gentleman who purchased G-Force."

Hector nodded, dropping Derek's hand and reaching out to shake Greg's. "That would be me. Although you might have heard we've been having some, er . . ."

Derek smiled, his teeth flashing straight and white beneath his shiny waxed mustache. "We are well aware of your difficulties, sir," he said with a nod. "In fact . . ." He looked expectantly at his brother.

Greg took the bait and nodded, turning to Hector with a grin. "That's sort of why we're here."

A wave of relief washed over Hector's face. "Does that mean you know where the girl could be?" he asked, gesturing to a pile of papers on his desk. I looked down and realized that he had been studying what looked like blueprints for the ride. "We've looked and looked and found nowhere for the girl to hide, but I noted that there might be space for a chamber here, or here, or here . . ." He pushed the papers toward us, pointing at several *X*s he'd marked in with red pencil.

But the Piperatos barely looked down. "There's no space inside G Force for someone to hide," Derek said brusquely. "We designed a thrill ride, not a place to store knickknacks."

Hector looked confused, but his confusion quickly turned to anger. "But the girl—"

Derek held up his hand as if to say *stop*. "We came here to discuss how to handle public relations moving forward," he said, reaching inside his jacket and pulling the smallest, thinnest laptop computer I'd ever seen from some inner pocket.

Hector turned to look at my brother and me with an expression of befuddlement, as if to say, *Are you guys seeing this?* I just nodded and watched Derek Piperato open up his tiny computer. He made a few clicks, then brought up a video. It was frozen on a photograph of two teenage girls riding a roller coaster, shrieking with delight.

"Public relations?" Hector asked finally, as if it had taken some effort to find his voice.

Greg nodded, flashing a bright white smile. "We couldn't help but notice that you're in a bit of a public relations jam," he explained. "The stories in the press are not . . . kind."

Hector widened his eyes. "No," he said, "because a young girl disappeared on your ride."

Derek waved his hand dismissively. *"Allegedly,"* he insisted. "She allegedly disappeared on our ride. How does everyone know she didn't sneak out before the lights came up? Maybe she had a boyfriend the parents disapproved of. Maybe she went *shopping.*"

Frank cleared his throat. "Um, that seems extremely unlike—"

But Derek cut him off. "Let's not speculate," he said. "The truth is, only the girl herself knows what happened. And the only thing we can control is how we react to our ride being attacked. Yes?"

He didn't wait for an answer before reaching down to the laptop and clicking on the video.

A deep, scary voice played over stock footage of young people screaming on amusement rides.

"You've heard about it on the news."

A quick shot of G-Force was shown, but too fast for the viewer to really make out what it was. The effect was a little disturbing.

"You've heard about it from your friends."

A shot of a teenage girl in the dark, a tear rolling down her face. Then three girls, whispering eagerly into one another's ears. Then a shot of a boy texting. Then . . .

"But are you brave enough to find out what really happened?"

A shot of the entrance to G-Force, with the line to get in snaking around the whole park. A grainy video of kids screaming, waving their I WAS FIRST TO RIDE G-FORCE T-shirts. A super-quick shot of one of its seats, restraints undone, sitting in the dark. The effect was weird and creepy—it looked almost like an electric chair.

"Are you brave enough to ride . . . the DEATH RIDE?"

The voice dissolved into a maniacal cackle as the camera jutted farther into G-Force, and the picture gave way to static, like a video feed cutting out.

There were a few seconds of creepy cackling over a black screen, then Funspot's logo and directions came up.

Greg and Derek turned to us eagerly. Frank, Hector, and I looked at one another in surprise. I don't think any of us knew what to say.

It was Hector who finally spoke. "What was *that*?" he demanded.

Derek, seemingly mistaking Hector's anger for enthusiasm, rubbed his hands together in excitement. "Isn't it magnificent? This was put together for us by Viral Genius, one of the foremost advertising firms in—"

Hector slammed his fist down onto his desk, and the room fell silent. "What do you think this is?" he demanded, glaring at the Piperato Brothers. "Is this a *joke* to you?"

Greg smoothed his mustache, looking offended. "Not at all," he said with a frown. "This is our livelihood and reputation on the line, as well as yours."

Derek looked angry now. "We *have* to control the conversation about what happened here last Saturday, or we're going to be the losers," he said, jabbing his finger at Hector for emphasis. "Really, Hector, it's Public Relations 101: Get ahead of the story."

Get ahead of the story. I'd heard that before, and I was pretty sure Derek was right: It was a big rule in public relations. But I was also pretty sure Hector was disgusted by the ad.

He gestured at the laptop. "What do you mean to do with that?" he asked. "Do you expect me to put it on TV? Because I won't."

Greg shook his head, smiling again. "You don't have to do anything, Hector. That's the beauty of our plan. You just sit back and watch the kids return. We've taken the liberty of placing this viral trailer on the Internet, where the kids are *already*—"

"What?" Hector asked, his eyebrows making angry points on his forehead. "You posted this somewhere without telling me?"

Greg gave a rueful smile. "Per our contract, when the park owner disagrees with us about the marketing of our creation, we have final say."

Hector groaned and closed his eyes. I could tell he remembered that part of the contract, and I could also tell he'd never thought such a situation would arise. In the silence that ensued, I moved forward, gesturing to the laptop.

"Can you play that again?" I asked the nearest Piperato brother—Derek.

"Gladly," he said, with the happy expression of someone who thought his brilliance was finally being appreciated. He clicked on the ad again, and it started up.

"You've heard about it on the news."

Stock footage. Creepy shot of the ride. Stock footage. Creepy shot . . .

I pointed at the shot of the ride with a line snaking around all of Funspot. "There—that had to be taken on Saturday night, right?"

That was the only time the line had been that long—or the people in it had looked so excited.

Derek nodded. "That's right."

Frank moved forward, his interest piqued. "Did you buy cell phone footage off someone in line or something?" he asked, squinting at the screen to get a better look.

Derek looked pleased. "It does look like that, doesn't it?" he asked proudly. "But actually, no, that's professional footage that's been given a filter to look more 'gritty' and 'immediate.' Studies show that modern teenagers respond more strongly—"

"Professional footage?" I asked, clicking on the touch pad to stop the trailer. "Does that mean you had someone shooting footage of the opening Saturday night?"

Greg stepped forward. "Sure," he said. "It's standard procedure to send a videographer to shoot the opening. You never know when a promotional opportunity might—"

Frank cut him off. "Do you have that footage with you?" he asked. "All of it?"

Greg and Derek glanced at each other, as if deciding how much they trusted us. Greg gave a slight nod, and Derek pursed his lips. Finally Derek turned back to us and spoke.

"We have a full DVD of footage," he said. "Probably an hour or more."

I practically jumped. *"Can we see it?"* I shouted, and at the brothers' perplexed expressions, tried to get ahold of myself. "Sorry. Can we see it? My brother and I are, ah . . ."

Hector spoke up in a calm, quiet voice. "The Hardy brothers are studying thrill ride design," he said smoothly, catching my eye and winking. That's when I remembered: We'd asked Hector not to tell anyone we were investigating this for him. I'd almost blown our cover.

Derek looked perplexed. "Well, that explains the third degree earlier," he said, nodding at Frank.

"I suppose we could let you borrow the footage," Greg went on, folding his arms in front of him. Then he cracked a small smile. "The Piperato Brothers of the future."

I had a sudden vision of Frank and me ten years from now, dressed in bow ties and fedoras, carrying computers the size of a deck of cards. I had to bite my lip to keep from laughing.

"Thanks. We really appreciate it," Frank was saying.

Hector stood. "I think this meeting is over," he said,

looking at the Piperatos. "In the future, I would appreciate it if you contacted me before placing any communication from Funspot anywhere."

"But we have the contract—" Greg tried to put in, but Hector cut him off, holding up his hand.

"A young girl disappeared here on Saturday night," he went on, in that same calm, quiet voice. "Do you have children, gentlemen?"

Derek and Greg looked at each other, confused. "We don't," Greg confirmed

Hector frowned. "Well, I have a daughter," he said. "And I can tell you that if anything ever happened to her—if she ever disappeared and I didn't know where she was—I don't know how I would survive it. I can't imagine what that poor girl's parents are going through right now. And the idea that they might see this viral whatever you put up, this—" He gestured to the laptop as though it were the most disgusting thing he'd ever seen. "This trailer. It disgusts me."

Greg and Derek exchanged a glance. Derek waited a moment before saying, "I'm sorry we disagree. But I think the trailer is brilliant. And once kids start crowding back into Funspot, I think you will too."

Hector sighed. "I think you should go."

Greg gave a quick nod, then folded up the laptop, turned to his brother, and gestured toward the door. "Here, kids," he said, slipping a small hard drive out of his pocket and handing it to me. "This has all the footage from the ride opening in a folder called 'G-Force.' I hope you learn from it."

I smiled. "Me too. Thanks."

The Piperato Brothers exited, and I turned to Hector. "Can we use your computer to—?"

He held up his hands. "Of course, of course." He sighed. "I think I'm going to take a coffee break. Will you boys be okay in here?"

"I think so," Frank said. I could tell by the way he was eyeing the hard drive that he was eager to get started.

"Good luck," Hector said as he walked out the door. From outside, I heard him add under his breath, "We all need it."

"That's Luke!" I cried a few minutes later, pointing at the screen as a black-shirted kid got out of line and walked out of the frame of the video.

Frank shook his head. "Sure enough," he said. We were watching footage of G-Force, right after the first ride had been boarded.

"Don't you think it's weird to get out of line when you're so close to the front?" I asked.

Frank nodded, his eyes still on the screen. The footage cut to a later scene, kids exiting the ride looking shaken. "It's definitely weird," he said, crossing his arms over his chest. The footage cut to Cal looking worried, then the police showing up. Then the camera panned back to the line, where kids looked both scared and disappointed.

Luke wasn't there, but the friends we'd seen him with last Saturday night were still in line.

"Maybe he got scared," I suggested. "You know, once Kelly's disappearance got out. Maybe he didn't want to risk going on a ride where someone went missing."

Frank shook his head. "No, that's not possible," he said, clicking the mouse to go back to the place where Luke stepped out of line. "See Cal closing up the ride there? Luke steps out before the ride even starts. It was way too early for him to know about Kelly."

I frowned. "Unless he knew about her . . . because he helped make her disappear."

5 BAD BREAKUPS

FRANK

UNLESS WHO HELPED MAKE HER DIS-appear?"

A female voice from the doorway made my head snap up. Joe and I had been so involved in watching the video that we hadn't even noticed Daisy walk in. She was watching us study the computer monitor, eyebrows furrowed.

Joe put on a goofy smile. "Oh . . . nothing," he said with a shrug. I shot my brother a look that said, *We're not telling her?* And he gave me a particular look back that I took to mean *Not yet.*

"We were just watching some footage of the ride, throwing out crazy theories," I said with a smile of my own. "We were just talking about . . . uh . . ." I tried to think of the least likely person to be involved in Kelly's disappearance. "Chief Olaf."

Chief Olaf is the new head of the Bayport PD. As far as his view of Joe's and my detective work goes . . . Well, let's just say that it ranges from just barely tolerant to grudging admiration, depending on what day of the week it is and exactly what Joe and I have been up to.

Daisy looked utterly confused. "That's interesting," she said, "because he just so happens to be here."

Joe turned bright red. "Now?" he asked.

Daisy smiled, noting his panicked expression. "Not right here," she said. "He and a few officers are waiting outside for Dad. They're taking a look at G-Force again, along with some inspectors."

"Oh." Joe's face took on its normal color again.

Daisy looked curious. "You didn't think he could really—?"

"No," I put in quickly, shaking my head. "Not at all. Just spouting crazy theories, like I said."

Daisy looked from me to Joe, not entirely sold. "You two have a very interesting way of working," she said. "Anyway—would you happen to know where my dad is?"

"He said he was getting coffee," I said.

"Ahhh." Daisy nodded. "Okay. I'll check the kitchen. Thanks."

She started to leave, but Joe called out, "Daisy?"

She turned. "Yes?"

Joe put on a very sweet smile. "Will you come back after you find him? We could hang out."

Daisy looked touched. "Okay, Joe. Sure. Be right back."

She walked out and back down the hallway, and I turned to my brother. "Should I go?" I asked, only half joking. "Am I a third wheel here?"

But Joe just shut down the video program and disconnected the hard drive, shaking his head. "Not that I wouldn't enjoy just hanging out with Daisy," he said, "but I thought we could ask her more about Luke."

That seemed like a good idea. It was only a few minutes until Daisy returned, pink-cheeked from running. "Hey, guys," she said, walking in and casually slinging herself into Hector's chair. "Man, I hope they find something. I haven't been sleeping much, I'm so worried about Kelly. . . ."

"Us too," I said. It was the truth. It had now been a full week since Kelly had disappeared, with no evidence, and no sign of her anywhere. Each day that passed made it less likely that a missing teenager would be found; Joe and I had been involved in crime fighting long enough to know that. And each day that passed made it harder to believe that there was a benign explanation for all this.

Daisy leaned back and closed her eyes. "I've been so stressed out," she said quietly. "Between what happened with Kelly and what it's doing to the park. This is so crazy."

Joe shot me an awkward sideways glance and cleared his throat. "Was it stressful seeing Luke again?" he asked, in a faux-casual voice.

Daisy opened her eyes and angled her head up to look at him. "Huh?"

Joe coughed. "Um, you know that guy Luke? He seemed kind of nasty."

Daisy looked from Joe to me, as if I held the explanation for Joe's strange questions.

I tried not to respond.

"Um," Daisy said, turning back to Joe, "I guess it was kind of stressful seeing Luke. He wasn't very nice to me, as you saw."

I tried to look sympathetic. "Why did you two break up? I mean, if you don't mind my asking."

Daisy looked surprised, but she didn't hesitate in her answer. "Actually, *I* broke it off with him."

I had to stop myself from shooting a look at Joe. *Motive!*

"Luke had been hoping that I'd get to attend Dalton Academy with him this fall—I mean, I had too." Daisy sighed.

Dalton Academy was a ritzy private school right on the outskirts of Bayport. Its students were regarded with a mixture of wonder and jealousy from us poor slobs at Bayport High. There were rumors of an indoor swimming pool beneath a retractable basketball court, kids who were helicoptered to school, and lobster Newburg in the cafeteria.

How much of that was true was anyone's guess.

"What happened?" asked Joe.

Daisy's expression soured for just a second, then quickly recovered. "My dad bought Funspot," she said in a resigned voice. "And then my mom got laid off. Suddenly we couldn't afford ice cream anymore—let alone some fancy private school."

She paused.

"It just got too hard with Luke after that," she said, shaking her head. "Going to different schools, and me trying to help my dad out with Funspot after school and on weekends. He wasn't, well—he wasn't very understanding."

"Luke wasn't?" I asked.

Daisy nodded. "He sent me a text right after we broke up saying that he hoped Funspot failed. He thought it was a stupid idea for my father to buy it. A lot of people did, actually." She sighed. "Maybe they were right."

Joe looked thoughtful. "Why was he at the opening, then?" he asked. "If he hates Funspot so much?"

Daisy shrugged. "I figured he was just being hotheaded and stupid when he sent me that text," she said. "He might think buying Funspot wasn't the best idea, but deep down he wants the best for me. Or so I'd like to think."

I looked at Joe. I could tell from his expression that we were thinking the same thing: *Or he showed up to sabotage G-Force—and Funspot.*

Suddenly we could hear voices arguing outside the administration building.

"How do you expect me to pay you early?"

Hector.

"I barely have enough cash to keep the park running on a day-to-day basis. Pay advances are off the table!"

"I'm in a real bind, or I wouldn't ask."

It took me a minute to identify the second voice—Cal.

"I just thought, under the circumstances—"

"Forget it." Hector cut Cal off. "I'm sorry, I would like to, but I can't. Don't ask again."

I couldn't help looking at Daisy, judging her reaction. If Hector was having difficulty meeting day-to-day expenses, then Funspot was in even worse trouble than we thought. A dark look flittered across Daisy's face, but she quickly stood up, putting on a neutral expression. "I'd better go help Dad," she said quietly.

Joe stood, and I followed his lead.

"We should go too," Joe said. "After about fifty rides on G-Force, I'm finally recovering my appetite."

Daisy looked amused. "You rode G-Force?"

Joe nodded. "About fifty times," he repeated. "At least, it felt like fifty times. How many times does it take to lose your ability to feel anything but pain?"

Daisy smiled. "For you? Maybe two? Three?"

Joe chuckled. "Well, I'll do anything to solve the case, my dear."

Daisy suddenly looked serious. "Did you find anything?" She looked hopefully from Joe to me.

I slowly shook my head.

"No," Joe said, putting his hand on Daisy's shoulder. "But we will. I promise. Okay?"

Daisy looked up at him and, after a moment, nodded. "Okay. Maybe we can hang out tomorrow night? I could use some time away from this park."

Joe smiled. "That sounds great. I'll text you."

We gathered our things, and Daisy led us out of the office and back out through the lobby to the park. Outside the building, Hector stood off to the left, talking on his cell phone, and Cal stood a few yards to the right, leaning against a tree and smoking a cigarette. He looked up when we came out; Hector seemed too involved in his phone call to notice us.

"Thanks for coming, guys," Daisy said, turning back to us with a weak smile. "Seriously, the only thing that got me out of bed this morning was the thought that you two are working on this, and with your help we might be able to reopen G-Force soon."

"It's our pleasure," I said sincerely. I tried to look away as Joe gave Daisy a hug and then my brother and I headed off toward the parking lot.

"Hey there, Miss Daisy," Cal said in his gravelly voice as we walked off. Daisy didn't respond, and after a moment, I turned back to see what she was doing.

"Did you hear me? I said hello." Cal dropped his cigarette butt and smashed it with his toe.

Daisy was standing near her father, staring off at the parking lot. Her jaw was clenched, and I could tell by her posture that she'd heard Cal and was struggling not to react.

After a few more seconds, Cal shook his head and ambled off in the direction of G-Force.

6

JOE

'M NO SORT OF HACKER, BUT IT WASN'T TER-
ribly hard to get into Dalton Academy's online student
directory. Within fifteen minutes of firing up my Internet
browser, I was looking at Luke Costigan's home address.

He lived in Hampton Estates, a fancy subdivision over
on the west side of town. So the next morning Frank and I
shoveled down six of Aunt Trudy's fresh raspberry ricotta
pancakes (with peach compote!) and jumped into the car to
drive across town.

"He's not going to talk to us," Frank predicted, looking full of either pancakes or malaise (or both). "He hates
us, remember? He saw us with his ex-girlfriend. He knows
you're dating her."

I turned the car onto Easthampton Drive. "It's worth a

shot," I said. "If he resists, we can pull the old 'need to use your bathroom' routine."

Frank seemed to perk up a little. "And find his cell phone or computer?" Frank grinned and pointed out the window. "Here we go," he said; "119 Easthampton Drive."

Luke Costigan's house was your typical suburban McMansion: huge, red brick, enormous bay windows, four-car garage. In the front, four Greek columns held up a generous porch. Two cars in the driveway implied that the family was home.

"Quick game plan?" asked Frank, but I was already unbuckling my seat belt.

"Ask questions," I said, pushing open the driver's-side door. "Hope nobody hits us."

Frank nodded. "And if all else fails, beg to use the bathroom?"

"Exactly."

I climbed out and ambled toward the front door, Frank falling into step beside me. When we'd climbed the front steps, I reached out and knocked an enormous door knocker in the shape of a bald eagle. We heard footsteps approaching the door, and then a middle-aged man answered.

"Can I help you?" he asked, not unfriendly.

"Actually, we were wondering if Luke is home?" Frank asked smoothly.

The man nodded. He had dark eyes and close-cropped

hair, like Luke, but unlike his son, his hair had gone mostly gray. "You two classmates from Dalton?" he asked.

"Um, we go to Bayport High," I replied. "But we have friends in common."

The man nodded, then stepped back into the house. "LUKE!" we heard him yell up the stairs. "You have friends at the door!"

"Who?" we heard a surly voice yell from upstairs, followed shortly (when his dad didn't answer) by footsteps on the carpeted stairs. Luke slowly became visible—first his feet, then his legs, then his shoulders—and when he was finally able to see us outside the door, he scowled.

"What are *you* doing here?" he asked as he ran up to the doorway.

"Who are they?" asked the man in a voice that sounded more curious than suspicious.

Luke narrowed his eyes at me. "This is Daisy's new boyfriend."

The man nodded. "Ahhhh," he said, not-so-slowly backing away. "Well, I'll leave you all to . . . talk?" He glanced at his son. "I'll be out in the garage if you need me."

Luke nodded, not taking his eyes off me.

Once his father had left the foyer, Luke scowled at us again. "What do you want?"

I crossed my arms in front of my chest. "We want to talk about what happened on G-Force last Saturday night."

Luke gave us a look like he thought we'd lost our minds. "How would I know?" he asked. "I didn't even ride the thing."

"But you were in line," Frank pointed out.

Luke cocked an eyebrow. "Yeeeeeah?" he asked, clearly not seeing a connection.

"And then you got *out* of line," I added. "Oddly enough, before the first ride even started."

Luke looked at Frank, then turned his glaring eyes on me. "So what?" he asked. "You guys were on the ride. Did *you* take her?"

Take her. So Luke knew what we were really accusing him of, which gave me an odd tremor in the pit of my stomach. Nobody really knew what had happened to Kelly. Did the fact that Luke used the words "take her" mean he knew more about it than he was letting on?

Frank glanced at me and said, "We didn't even know Kelly was missing until a few minutes after the ride ended." He paused. "As we were saying, though—it's kind of strange to leave the line when you're so close to the front, don't you think?"

Luke frowned. "Why?"

I sighed. I hate it when people are obstinate. "Because one would assume you were excited to ride something you'd waited hours to board, yet you suddenly walked away like you'd changed your mind. Did you?"

"Change your mind?" Frank added.

Luke sighed now, shaking his head. "Why are you guys asking? What are you, the FBI?"

I glanced at Frank. "We're people who care about finding Kelly," I said simply.

Luke frowned. There wasn't much he could say to that. Argue with us, and it would seem like he didn't care about finding the missing girl.

He looked past us, down the driveway. "My buddies sent me out," he said. "They bet me twenty bucks I couldn't figure out what the thing did. So I walked around it, but they were right, man—" He stopped and chuckled ruefully. "I couldn't figure out a thing. It looks like a spaceship, right?"

Frank nodded, relaxing his expression a little.

"And it doesn't even look like it's moving from the outside," Luke added. "I was stumped. So I finally gave up."

I nodded. "But you didn't get back in line," I pointed out.

Luke turned to me, glaring again. "How do you know all this?"

"Someone took a video," Frank said simply, not explaining further. Luke would probably think someone shot the line with their cell phone camera—which was fine.

Luke was quiet for a moment. It made me nervous. When someone you're questioning goes quiet, it usually means they're thinking. And when the person you're questioning is thinking, it means that they could, at any moment, arrive at the discovery that they really don't have to answer your questions. After all, Frank and I are just kids like Luke—not cops or the FBI.

It was time to turn up the heat.

"Daisy says you two had a pretty nasty breakup," I pointed out.

Luke looked at me again. "She said that?" he asked, sounding a little hurt.

"She said you texted her saying you wanted Funspot to fail," I added.

Luke shook his head and let out an angry chuckle. "I *did* want it to fail," he said. "That piddly, pathetic little amusement park broke us up. Her father and his stupid ideas!"

"What do you mean?" asked Frank. We knew what he meant, of course, but it's always good to keep your subject talking.

Luke turned to Frank. "Her father spent all his money on Funspot," he said. "Suddenly there's no money to send Daisy to Dalton with me, like she'd planned. Next thing I know, she breaks up with me. 'It's just too hard,' she says, 'going to different schools.'" He snorted. "You believe that?"

"It just seems like if you wanted Funspot to fail badly enough," I said, "you might do something to sabotage it."

Luke turned his eyes back to me. I could see him trying to make sense of what I'd said—and once he got it, fury burned in his eyes. "Sabotage?" he repeated. "You think I'd kidnap some girl to get back at Daisy? That's sick!"

"Maybe you didn't kidnap her," I suggested. "Maybe you made a deal with her to hide somewhere, to make it look like she disappeared on the ride. But what I'm saying—"

Luke held up his hand, cutting me off. "I don't care what you're saying!" he shouted. "I wouldn't hurt some kid to get back at Daisy, okay?" He glared at me one last time, then turned away, like he was trying to cool off.

"So why didn't you get back in line?" Frank asked neutrally.

Luke groaned and turned back around. "I got scared, okay? When those doors opened, I realized I didn't want to get on. So I told my buddies I had to use the bathroom, and I took off."

I looked at Frank. *Scared? This guy?* "Really?" I asked.

Luke scowled. "Yes, really!"

I turned back to Luke and just stared at him for a moment. He seemed tense. Not necessarily lying-tense, but . . . "No offense," I said, "but why should I believe you?"

Luke groaned again. He looked at the ceiling. "I hate it when people say 'no offense' when they're about to insult you," he muttered.

"No offense," I said again. I knew it sounded like a line. But I meant it.

Luke closed his eyes, then looked back at me. "I actually have someone who can back me up," he said after a few seconds. "Someone who works at the park saw me. My neighbor. You know Jamie King?"

• • •

All things being equal, Jamie King was not someone I would choose to involve in an investigation. Discretion-wise, she's kind of—how do I say this?—a nightmare. I could only imagine that Jamie, not unlike Frank and me, keeps her ear to the ground and soaks up information like a sponge. But while Frank and I like to then hang out on the side of the sink, quietly absorbing all our spongy information, Jamie likes to squeeze herself out all over the nearest classmate.

I guess what I'm trying to say is that Jamie King is a gossip queen.

But we needed her to back up Luke's alibi. If he really had left the G-Force line because he got scared, then he wasn't much of a suspect. And that meant we had to look in another direction.

"Oh, heeeeyyy!" Jamie greeted us with a smile when she opened the door, not looking surprised at all. I wondered if classmates just dropped by her house every Sunday. "It's the Hardy Boys! What's up, dudes?"

Before we could respond, her expression turned serious, and she leaned toward us like she was asking us something personal. "Have you guys talked to Daisy?" she asked. "Is she, like, all right?"

Frank started up, "Well, she's—"

But I cut him off. "She's fine," I said curtly, shooting Frank a *Zip it!* look. I had a feeling that whatever we shared with Jamie would be all over Bayport within hours. And while she and Daisy were friendly, I wanted to let Daisy decide how much of the whole G-Force debacle she wanted to make public knowledge.

"Actually," I went on, "we have some questions for *you*."

Jamie blinked her big blue eyes at us. "*Moi?*" she asked, putting a hand to her chest.

"*Vous*," I replied. (That's right. I didn't get a B-minus in French 101 for nothing!) "It's pretty simple, really. Did you see Luke Costigan last Saturday night, around the time of the first G-Force ride?"

Jamie's eyes widened. "Did I!" She leaned in confidentially. "You guys, he was like, *terrified*." She shook her head. "I was on my break and at the coin toss booth—just for fun, you know? And right next door is the ball toss? And those guys, like, the guys who run it, they really *insult* people to get them to play, especially guys. You know?"

My brain was working overtime trying to follow. But yes—I thought I knew. "Yes?" I said.

"So one of them called after him, 'Hey, Preppy Boy, what's wrong, you too scared to ride the big bad spaceship?' And he turned around—and I know Luke, you guys, he doesn't stand for stuff like that usually—and his face was just *white*. And he saw me and was like, 'Where's the bathroom?' And I was like, 'Are you okay?' And he goes, 'Yeah, where's the bathroom?' so I told him."

I looked at Frank. So Luke was telling the truth.

Which meant we still had no idea who was behind whatever happened to Kelly.

I saw his shoulders droop slightly and knew he had come to the same conclusion.

Jamie continued. "Listen, you guys, if I were you? I would look into that creepy carnie guy, Cam or Can or whatever his name is. . . ."

"Cal?" I asked.

She nodded emphatically. "My friend Katie? She works the nacho booth? She says he was totally weird to her one time when he ordered nachos. He was all like, 'No jalapeños!' and she was like, 'Um, they're *in the sauce*,' and he got all flustered, like he'd never heard of nacho sauce before. And she said when she gave him the nachos, he reached up and his sleeves fell down and his *arms* were, like, *covered* with track marks." She paused, gauging our reaction, and then leaned forward. "Like for *drugs*," she added.

I was silent for a moment, mentally calculating the likelihood that Cal used drugs versus the likelihood that Jamie was exaggerating the truth in order to have something to talk about. I doubted Hector would have hired Cal if he used drugs, and I recalled Daisy saying that they drug-tested all job applicants. Still, it was something we could look for the next time we saw Cal.

Seeming unsatisfied with our reaction—or lack thereof—Jamie huffed and crossed her arms. "He also takes the *bus* to work," she said. "I mean, who takes the bus?"

I knew the answer to that one, and it was: people who can't afford a car. It's pretty simple, really. But I was getting the feeling maybe Jamie just didn't like Cal, so I didn't see the point in giving her Bus 101.

"Did you actually see Cal do anything weird on the night of the incident?" Frank asked, trying to get us back on a logical track.

Jamie looked from Frank to me, and her eyes flashed with annoyance. I could tell she didn't like our reaction to her dirt on Cal. But after a moment, she nodded. "Yeah," she said. "In fact, I did."

She paused, waiting for us to ask her, and Frank finally did. "What did you see?" he asked.

Jamie straightened up. "He left his post," she said, "while the ride was running."

"Where did he go?" I asked.

Jamie shrugged. "I don't know," she said. "I just looked over at the booth while the ride was going, and he was gone."

Hmm. I wasn't sure what to make of Jamie's tip. She clearly didn't like Cal, and it was possible he'd left the booth for a totally normal reason—checking something on the ride, for example. Still, I filed it away. I remembered Daisy's strange behavior toward Cal the morning before. It wasn't like her to be rude.

"Well, thanks a lot for the information," Frank said with a nod. "We really appreciate it. I guess we'll see you at school?"

Jamie nodded slowly. Her expression implied that she wasn't sure what to make of us. I felt sure she was used to a more appreciative audience for her gossip. After a few seconds she shrugged, and the apprehension was gone from her face.

"See you guys around," she said lightly, and closed the door.

As we walked back to our car—still parked in front of Luke's house—my phone beeped with an incoming text.

I pulled it out and held the screen so Frank could see. It was from Daisy.

GOOD NEWS . . . THE INSPECTORS & POLICE STILL CAN'T FIND ANYTHING WRONG WITH THE RIDE, SO G-FORCE REOPENS TONIGHT.

TAKEN FOR A RIDE

7

FRANK

"OH . . . WOW," MY BROTHER SAID AS we pulled into the parking lot for Funspot that evening. "Are you seeing this?"

Dusk was just falling, and the lights of the carnival rides blinked in an enticing rhythm. But to my surprise, we weren't going to be able to park all that close to them.

Because the parking lot was *packed*!

"Seriously?" I looked at Joe in surprise. "Why? I mean, I'm happy for Daisy, but . . ."

I drove the car down a long lane of parked cars, looking for a space. Teenagers clustered around cars and strolled toward the long lines at the ticket booths, chatting excitedly. Our windows were down, so every so often I caught a few words.

". . . don't know if I'm brave enough to ride it . . ."

". . . didn't really *die*, right?"

". . . nobody knows what happened to her . . ."

". . . have to check out the Death Ride . . ."

My mouth dropped open. I looked at Joe, who looked just as flabbergasted as I felt.

"The trailer!" we both cried at the same time.

This had to be the work of the trailer the Piperato Brothers had made, calling G-Force the "Death Ride." It had never really occurred to me that the trailer might *work*. I guess I never got past it being extremely poor taste to use the disappearance of a young girl as a marketing angle. Besides, didn't the trailer basically say, "Come to Funspot and ride G-Force and you might die"? Who saw that and thought, *Yes, please?*

Who *were* these people?

Joe caught my eye and seemed to grasp my confusion. "Well . . . according to my biology class, teenagers' brains aren't fully developed yet. The unfinished parts seem to control judgment and, um, making good decisions."

I pulled into the first open parking space I saw, at least half a mile from the ticket booths.

"Teenagers also seem to view themselves as invincible," Joe went on. "So I guess, when you challenge them with a Death Ride, the most common response would be . . . ?"

"'I gotta get on that thing,'" I replied, quoting a red-haired kid we'd just passed a few seconds ago.

Joe nodded. "Yeah," he said.

I put the car in park and took the keys out of the ignition. The engine died, and we just sat there for a minute or two, listening to the excited chatter all around us.

"You realize we're both teenagers," I said finally.

Joe nodded. "Maybe we have really quick-developing brains?" he said.

I shook my head and climbed out of the car. Joe followed, and we made the long trek to the ticket booths, where Daisy had instructed us to bypass the lines, go to the 'will call' booth, and ask for her. We did, and a few minutes later Daisy came to get us—pink-cheeked and happy-looking.

"Do you *believe* this?" she asked, gesturing to the lines.

Joe nodded. "It's crazy. Is your dad excited?"

Daisy bit her lip. "I think he doesn't know how to feel," she replied. "On the one hand, we might be able to afford groceries this week. But on the other, Kelly's still missing. . . ."

"Yeah," Joe said, looking out over the lines. "It's hard to know how to react."

"It has to be that trailer the Piperato Brothers made," I suggested. "Right?"

Daisy nodded. "Yeah. They're here, and they're super excited. I guess the video went viral and has been viewed some crazy number of times . . . a hundred thousand? Maybe even more?"

I looked back at the lines snaking back from the ticket booths almost halfway through the parking lot. I could swear I could even hear the trailer playing on people's smartphones. *"You've heard about it on the news . . ."*

"Well," I said after a moment. "I guess if we can't beat 'em . . ."

Joe smiled. "Should we head over to G-Force?"

Daisy nodded eagerly. "I think they're going to let in the first ride soon."

It was hard to know what to think as we watched Cal load the first set of riders into G-Force. (Joe, Daisy, and I were watching from the dining area off to the right—we'd decided to sit it out and observe.) Cal seemed to take extra long to strap everyone in and run the mandatory safety checks. I couldn't help glancing at his arms, which were bare in his short-sleeved motorcycle T-shirt, but I didn't see any sign of the track marks Jamie had mentioned. I wondered if Jamie had a reason to want us to suspect Cal, or whether she just flat-out didn't like him.

But more than anything, as we watched Cal fire up the controls and the ride hummed into action, I found myself thinking about Kelly Keohane. Fourteen years old is not that old. It's not old enough to drive a car, or drop out of school, or do a lot of the things that older kids do to show the adults in their lives that *they're* in control. It seemed way too young to run off with a boyfriend, or even a BFF. Besides, none of Kelly's friends claimed to have any idea where she was. She'd just disappeared. Like into thin air.

Was it really possible that this was something she'd planned—that she was somewhere safe and happy?

It was getting harder and harder to believe that, and yet life was going on right in front of us.

As the first G-Force ride came to a stop and the doors opened up, the Piperato Brothers stepped up onto the ride platform, holding a bullhorn. I could see Hector off to the side, looking pained. Cal emerged from G-Force and said something to Derek Piperato, who held the bullhorn to his lips and yelled, "Everyone present and accounted for!"

The crowd went nuts, cheering, and then, after a few seconds, a few wise guys started to boo.

"What," I asked out loud, "you *wanted* someone else to disappear?"

But Derek put the bullhorn back to his lips and announced, "The Death Ride has failed to claim a second victim. Who's brave enough to ride it next?"

The line started cheering again. The first riders streamed out, looking dazed but happy, and Cal made his way to the ride entrance and let in another twenty or so people.

Daisy let out an uneasy chuckle. "I feel like a huge boulder was just lifted off my shoulders," she said quietly. "As lame as that is. I was so nervous!"

Joe put his hand on her shoulder. "You know Frank and I rode the ride about twenty times and nothing happened," he assured her.

"Except that you puked," I pointed out.

Joe shot me an exaggerated glare. "Hey, Frank, why don't you get us all some lemonade or something?"

Daisy smiled. "Actually, that's not a bad idea. Here, show them this." She handed me a Funspot ID card with her photo on it. "Ask them to put it on my tab."

I took the card and obeyed, taking my time meandering from food stand to food stand, looking for the best lemonade. (Logic told me they were probably all made from the same mix, but I was trying to take my time.) As I wandered, G-Force took in and let out another group . . . then another . . . then another. Each time the ride ran and nothing unusual happened, Derek Piperato made a pithy little announcement and the crowd whooped. After the fifth ride, Derek announced that a new item was available in the Funspot gift shops: I SURVIVED THE DEATH RIDE T-shirts. He held one up. The front showed a caricature of a girl screaming with the slogan printed in huge, horror-movie-style letters.

"Gross," I muttered, loading the three lemonades into a cardboard carrier and making my way back to Joe and Daisy.

As I got closer, I caught sight of the two of them and wondered whether I should have tried to dawdle even more. Their heads were bent close together, and they were deep in conversation. I was getting the feeling that Joe really liked this girl. I clutched my lemonade and looked around for a distraction, but before I could find one, I heard, "Frank! Hey, awesome, you got the lemonade."

I looked up to see Daisy waving me over, a warm smile on her face. I smiled back. I knew she was trying to make me feel included, and I appreciated it.

I walked over, catching the tail end of my brother's question: ". . . on purpose, then? Do you know something about him?"

Daisy shrugged, and it occurred to me that she might actually have waved me back to avoid whatever Joe was asking her about.

As Cal let the next group in, the line moved up, and a familiar face stepped out of line toward us.

"Well, well, well," Luke smirked. "If it isn't Daisy and her new boyfriend, Sherlock Holmes."

"You came back to ride the ride," I replied flatly. "Are you feeling braver today?"

A flutter of annoyance passed across Luke's face. "You talked to Jamie, then? She told you the truth?"

Daisy was looking back and forth between Luke, Joe, and me, like she didn't understand what was going on. She pulled her dainty eyebrows together, a deep crease forming in the middle. Was she upset?

"What are you guys talking about?" she asked.

Joe turned to her. "It's nothing." Then he looked back at Luke. "Yeah, Jamie backed up your story," he said, sounding not so happy about it. "You got too scared to ride the ride, and you had to pee. Thanks for being honest with us."

Luke glared at him, but any reply he might have made

was cut off by Daisy putting up her hand and leaning forward.

"Hold on," she said, looking from me to Joe. "Did you two go question Luke about G-Force or something?"

Luke let out a caustic laugh. "Yeah, they thought I kidnapped Kelly to get back at you. Sounds totally reasonable, right?"

Daisy made a face like she smelled something terrible. "Seriously?" she asked, looking at Joe.

Joe sighed. He shrugged. I could tell he was uncomfortable. But what could we have done? We were working for Daisy, and that meant getting to the bottom of what happened with G-Force. It didn't mean asking her permission to question her ex-boyfriend or anyone else.

Joe still wasn't saying anything, and Luke took advantage of his momentary silence.

"What do you say, Daze—wanna ride with me?" He gestured toward the ride, where Cal was letting in yet another group. The line was moving forward. Luke would be on the next ride.

Daisy smiled at him, and for a moment I could see that they had been boyfriend and girlfriend. Her expression was full of fondness, with no trace of the annoyance I'd seen the week before. I got a nagging feeling in the pit of my stomach. Was this bad news for Joe?

Then Daisy bit her lip. "Oh, but we haven't been waiting in line," she said.

Luke rolled his eyes in an exaggerated way. "Daze, your father owns the park," he pointed out. "I think you could pull some strings."

Daisy smiled again and got to her feet. For a minute I thought she was just going to walk off with Luke and leave us there, but then she turned around.

"You guys wanna come too?"

I could tell that Joe was about to say no—whether from hurt feelings or a genuine desire to keep his lemonade down, I couldn't say. I nodded fiercely. "*Yes*," I said, hauling Joe up by the arm and purposely walking forward.

Luke frowned, but shrugged at Daisy, who glanced back at us briefly before leading the way up to the front of the line.

"What was that about?" Joe hissed at me as Daisy walked up to Cal and started gesturing.

"Research," I hissed back. "We need to go on this thing again. And I want to keep an eye on Luke."

Joe winced, still watching Daisy. "For me or for the case?" he asked.

"Both," I answered honestly. "Hey—what were you two talking about when I came back? It seemed a little tense for a minute."

Joe frowned, then seemed to remember. "Oh, I asked her about Cal," he whispered. Daisy had now stepped back from the ride operator, who was watching G-Force wind down. "Get this—her dad told her to stay away from him."

I raised an eyebrow. "Hector? But he had only glowing things to say about Cal the other morning."

Joe nodded. "I know; it's weird, right? I tried to press her for details, but all she would say was that it was awkward and she didn't totally understand it."

A stream of people exited the ride, all chatting excitedly and whooping. One guy turned in my direction and randomly gave me the "Rock on!" sign.

"Glad you liked it," I said, nodding.

Daisy came over and touched Joe's arm. "Come on, guys," she said. "We're skipping the line. Let's hurry so no one notices."

Cal was standing by the exit gate of G-Force, and he nodded and quickly waved us in. Then he took us around to the front of the line and gestured to the open door. Joe and I definitely knew the drill by now, so we all rushed in and chose seats in a row at the far side of the circle.

As we all buckled in, I saw Joe reach over and touch Daisy's shoulder.

"Hey," he whispered. "I'm sorry we didn't tell you. I didn't want to upset you, and it turned out to be nothing."

Daisy gave him a long look before her expression warmed a bit. "Okay," she whispered. "It's just, you're doing this as a favor to me. I thought you would keep me posted."

Joe nodded. "I will from now on. Okay?"

Other riders were streaming in through the door now, and Daisy's answer was lost in the noise from the crowd.

While the new riders got settled, I carefully pulled my smart-phone out of my jeans pocket and lifted it to look at its face.

That afternoon, in anticipation of riding G-Force again, I'd downloaded a "night vision" app and installed it. I wasn't sure how it would work with all the flashing lights and projections, but I figured it was worth a shot.

I got it set up and started recording as Cal strapped in the last rider and headed out the door.

"Enjoy, kids," he called behind him.

In the seconds before the ride started up, I glanced at my brother. He looked like he was steeling himself. Then I caught a glance at Luke, two seats away on the other side of Daisy. He was staring forward, with a determined expression, like he was trying to psych himself up.

Was I the only one looking forward to this?

The opening chords of "Beautiful" started up, and we were plunged into darkness. Several people screamed, clearly having their first G-Force experience. I struggled to keep my smartphone up and recording the action, but it was hard. The music, the lights, and the images took over. Soon I was totally disoriented, lost in the experience.

After a few minutes the images slowed and the ride began circling again, losing speed. The song finished up. Soon the circle of seats slid to a stop. Gradually, the purple lights dimmed on.

One of the newbies started cheering, and others soon joined in. I checked my hand—yep, I was still clutching my smartphone, camera side out. I reached up and clicked off the recording. Maybe this would give us some important information about how G-Force ran.

Suddenly I heard Daisy screaming.

"Oh my God! Oh my *God*! He was right here!"

I turned around. Joe was holding her hand, trying to comfort her, as they both leaned over . . .

An empty seat, with the restraints cut.

Luke was gone.

THE DEATH RIDE STRIKES AGAIN

8

JOE

"NO, I TOLD YOU. I DIDN'T HEAR ANYTHING," Daisy was telling Chief Nelson Olaf for the third time. "The ride was way too loud. The first time I noticed anything was wrong was when the ride was over—I looked over and his seat was empty."

I squeezed her hand. We were sitting in hard plastic chairs in Hector's office. After Luke's disappearance, it had taken the cops only minutes to show up.

Almost like they'd been worried about something like this.

Chief Olaf nodded, tapping the end of his pen to his lips.

"Did they find anything in the ride?" I broke in. "Any trace of a struggle? Did they fingerprint yet?"

Olaf frowned at me and wagged his pen in my direction. "Pipe down, Hardy."

I wondered if he could tell Frank and me apart, or whether we mingled in his mind into one big distasteful blob labeled "Hardy." Tip #1 for Unlicensed Investigators: Law enforcement will not like you. You think you're trying to do them a favor; they think you're trying to make them look bad.

Olaf turned back to Daisy. "As I was saying before I was so rudely interrupted. Was Luke having any problems at home that you know of?"

I groaned. I couldn't help it. Olaf had asked Daisy this five times—each time, the answer was no. I was getting the uncomfortable feeling that in the absence of a real explanation, Olaf was going to paint a "the kid was troubled and ran away somehow" explanation on this case.

Which would not serve Luke any better than it was serving poor Kelly.

Daisy sighed loudly. "*No,*" she said for the fifth time.

Olaf looked at me, his annoyed expression implying that I'd somehow put her up to that answer. He slapped his pen down onto the table and started rifling through his notebook. "I'll need you to step out so I can question the lady alone, Hardy," he said.

I tried not to roll my eyes. Like not having me around would make Daisy answer his questions any differently. And the cops were wasting time in here, asking the same questions over and over again when they could be out looking for clues.

But I had no legal right to stay; I knew that. I stood and shot Daisy a supportive glance. "See you soon," I said, and walked out of the office.

Downstairs, Frank and Hector were standing in the lobby, shuffling around restlessly like they couldn't relax enough to sit still. The door to another room was closed, and I could hear muffled voices within.

"Who's in there?" I asked, jabbing a thumb at the second office.

Hector looked up. "An officer is questioning Cal," he replied, then quickly averted his eyes. As I was about to turn to my brother, I caught Hector looking back at the closed door, a strange look in his eyes. Was it concern? Fear?

I remembered what Daisy had told me about Cal and nudged Frank.

"Hey, Hector," I said, "is there anywhere we can speak privately?"

Hector looked at me, then across the room to the various security guards, witnesses, and cops who were hanging around. The Piperato Brothers were draped across a few plastic chairs beneath a window, apparently snoozing while they awaited their turn to be questioned. Hector nodded and gestured to the front door. "Let's go outside. I could use some fresh air."

He led the way out the door, and Frank and I followed. Outside, it was eerily quiet; all the rides and games had been turned off when the park was closed hours ago, and most of the employees—any of them not directly involved with G-Force—had been sent home. Some of the lights on the rides still blinked silently.

There is nothing creepier than an abandoned amusement park.

Hector sighed and rubbed his eyes. It was getting late, well past midnight. But I could tell that Hector's weariness ran much deeper than the late hour. He looked like a man who literally didn't know what to do anymore. I couldn't imagine how it must feel to gamble your whole family's future on a new ride and have this happen.

Hector gestured for us to follow him down the midway, where, when the park was open, hawkers would beckon guests to try their luck on shooting games, darts, and roll-the-ball horse-race games. Now the booths were dark, and every so often I caught the white of a fake horse's or clown's eye glowing from within.

"I wanted to ask you about Cal," I said finally, when we were a good distance from the offices.

Hector looked surprised. "Cal? What do you want to know?"

I glanced at Frank, who was watching eagerly. "Do you trust him?" I asked.

Hector looked surprised, but deep in his eyes, I saw something else—recognition. He knew we were onto something. "Do I trust Cal? Well, I hired him, didn't I? Would I hire someone I didn't trust?"

Frank cocked an eyebrow. "Would you?" he asked. "Or maybe the better question is—why would you?"

Hector looked from my brother to me. "I don't understand," he said.

I sighed. "I noticed that Daisy was a little strange with him the other day," I explained. "When I asked her about it, she said you told her to stay away from him. That doesn't sound like something you'd say about a person you trust."

Hector's eyes widened, then he looked down at the ground. When he looked back up, he was wearing an expression of forced calm. "It's not a big deal," he said, with a little shrug. "I guess I'm overprotective of my little girl. At least, that's what she tells me!"

He laughed, but when neither Frank nor I smiled back, he stopped abruptly.

"Why would you need to protect her from Cal?" Frank asked quietly.

Hector looked down. "It's not a big deal. Just a dad's paranoia."

I was getting frustrated. "About *what*?" I asked.

Hector sighed and looked up at me. "Cal had a rough childhood. He has—well—he has a bit of a rap sheet."

"What's on it?" asked Frank. I was wondering too. There's a big difference between a history of misdemeanors or even burglaries and a history of violent crime. The former wouldn't make Cal all that scary. The latter . . . well . . .

But why would Hector hire a guy with a history of violent crime?

"It's all older stuff," Hector said. "Burglaries mostly, some stolen cars."

"How long ago are we talking?" I asked.

Hector shrugged. "At least ten years."

Now I was really feeling confused. "So why would you tell Daisy to avoid him? It seems like he's gotten his life back together."

Hector pressed his lips together. "Well," he said after a moment, "there was this little something that happened on his last job."

I raised my eyebrows beseechingly. *What?*

Hector went on. "He, well, he was fired from working at the big Five Pennants park for this little incident with a coworker." He shrugged again. "She said he threatened her when she made a joke about his missing teeth. Flew off the handle, told her she had no idea what kind of life he'd led and he'd show her hard times. . . ."

I looked at Frank. *Yikes!*

"And this coworker . . . was she another adult?"

Hector frowned. "No," he said. "She was a teenager."

"Did he actually attack her?" I asked.

Hector shook his head. "Other coworkers broke it up," he said. "One big guy led him away and calmed him down. Cal says it was nothing—he never would have hurt her. He was just angry, he says. He just needed to yell."

I looked at Frank. People who just need to yell usually don't make specific threats. People who make specific threats usually mean their target harm—even if only in the moment.

I remembered what Jamie had told us about Cal leaving his post when Kelly went missing. Was it possible she was telling the truth? Did Cal, in fact, have a dark side?

"Can you clear something up for me?" Frank asked, tilting his head as he looked at Hector. "I'm confused. Why would you hire a guy you don't trust around your daughter . . . to work in an *amusement park*?"

Good point. I examined Hector's face. He began sputtering, waving his hands like we were making too big a deal out of this.

"It's not that I don't *trust* him," he said, shaking his head like that was a crazy interpretation. "I never said that. I just . . . it's not just Cal, really. Daisy can be a firecracker. You probably know that as well as anybody. . . ."

He looked at me and laughed feebly. I didn't laugh back. Daisy had her moments, sure, but if Hector was implying that she might set off an otherwise harmless man into harming her somehow, I couldn't get behind that.

Hector shook his head. "Forget what I said earlier. Of course I trust Cal. Everyone deserves a second chance, and I'm glad I was able to give him that. Maybe Daisy misinterpreted what I said. I don't remember what I told her, exactly. Anyway . . ."

He looked around, as if desperately looking for a way out of this conversation.

As fate would have it, an exit door was approaching—in the form of Chief Olaf.

The chief walked toward us and sighed deeply. "I think we've got what we need. Hector, you can close up the park. Let's all go home and get some sleep."

"Did you find any leads?" Frank asked eagerly. "Any evidence of Luke in the park, after he rode G-Force?"

Chief Olaf turned to him and narrowed his eyes. "That's confidential information," he said, "and to be honest, I'm still not entirely clear on what you two boys have been doing hanging around Funspot so often. It seems you've spent quite a bit of time here since the first disappearance, according to witnesses."

Hector coughed loudly, then laughed. "Joe here has been seeing my daughter Daisy." He put his arm around my shoulders and smiled. "He seems like a nice young man, but I don't know why they need to spend so much time together! They're so young! But who can stand in the way of young love, eh?"

The chief looked skeptically from Hector to me, but then smiled. "My daughter's only eight, so I wouldn't know yet," he said. "I'll take your word for it, Hector. I will say that there are certainly much worse boys in this town that your daughter could choose to spend her time with."

Hector smiled again. "Yes, these are good boys." He

pulled his arm away and stepped back. "Shall we get our things and go, boys? I'm sure we're all tired."

I nodded. "Yeah, it's pretty late."

Chief Olaf led the way back to the administration building, and Hector, Frank, and I fell into step behind him.

"I don't think I'm going to get much sleep tonight," Frank muttered, casting a glance back in the direction of G-Force.

"Me neither," Hector said gravely.

I turned his words over and over in my mind as we said our good-byes, and then took the long walk back to our car.

Was Hector going to have trouble sleeping because two kids were still missing?

Or was he going to have trouble sleeping because deep down, he knew who'd taken them?

SECRETS 9

FRANK

IT HAD BEEN A LONG, LONG NIGHT, BUT SLEEP was not in my forecast when we got home. Instead I pulled out my smartphone and held it up to Joe.

"Secret weapon," I said, walking into my room and hooking it up to my computer.

Joe stumbled after me, looking very sleepy. "What do you mean?"

I woke up my computer and then clicked on a video-viewing program that would allow us to see the footage on the monitor. "Remember that night-vision app I down-loaded? I used it to film our G-Force ride tonight."

Joe raised an eyebrow, suddenly looking more alert. "You filmed the ride where Luke disappeared?"

I nodded. "I tried to, anyway. I don't know how sharp the video will be—it was hard to hold the phone straight with the ride in motion. But it's worth a shot."

A *ding* sounded to tell us that the video had uploaded to the computer, and I double-clicked to start it.

The footage started out clear, with the other riders visible, lined up across from me in their seats. Once the ride started, though, it got pretty blurry and shaky. I could make out figures moving through the frame, carried by the ride, but just like being on G-Force, it was hard to tell exactly what I was looking at or what was moving where.

Joe groaned. "This is making me queasy."

I tried to stay focused on the figures onscreen, looking for any sudden, weird movements that might be related to Luke's disappearance. So far I didn't see anything. Then all of a sudden, the motion slowed and the figures slowly circled back into place.

Soon a full row of seats slowed to a halt across from the camera.

The lights came up, and the video ended.

"I got nothing," Joe said, sounding sleepy again.

I shrugged. "Maybe there's nothing to get," I said. "This isn't exactly a professional-quality video."

Joe yawned. "It was a good idea to take it, though. Listen, I need to get some shut-eye."

I nodded, my eyes never leaving the screen. "Go to bed, Joe. I'll see you in the morning."

My brother lingered behind me. "You're staying up?" he asked.

I shook my head. "Not for long. I just want to watch this a couple more times . . . see if anything jumps out at me."

"Okay." Joe's footsteps slowly headed out the door. "Wake me if you notice anything."

"I will." Joe shut my bedroom door and headed down the hall to his room.

The house was nearly silent. I cued the video to play again . . . then again. Then one more time. Each time, as the riders spun to a stop, I told myself I would only watch it once more. I needed sleep, after all. But somehow I couldn't tear my eyes away. I felt like this video had something to tell me—something I just couldn't make out yet.

I finally shut my eyes, but was still restless. I know I must have fallen asleep, because I had a terrifying dream: Someone had pushed me off the Funspot Ferris wheel and I was hanging on to Joe for dear life! I woke up soaked in sweat.

Soon pale light was shining through my windows, and I could hear the calls of birds waking up to search for food. In an hour or so Joe would be up. I'd given up my chance of getting any real sleep that night.

But then I saw it. A crouched shape moving just *behind* the row of seats. It seemed to come up from the floor. Just as quickly as it appeared, it vanished, darting off to the left.

I replayed that section of video. Was I just so tired I was seeing things? But no, it was real. A person—sneaking into the ride as it was in motion. It was impossible to make out features, but the figure looked too tall to be Luke himself.

It was more the size of a tall, skinny grown man.

A tall, skinny grown man like Cal Nevins.

It was Monday, and Joe and I were due at school in just an hour or so. But instead of eating Aunt Trudy's sweet potato pancakes and leisurely getting ready, we threw on clothes, grabbed a couple of granola bars, and jumped into the car.

Hector had mentioned that the ride inspectors were coming back this morning, and Joe and I wanted to be there.

Funspot was still closed, so we parked right near the service entrance and waved at the security guard, who recognized us by now. He let us into the employees-only area, which was bustling with activity. The ride inspectors had just arrived, and Hector was getting ready to lead them out to G-Force. Daisy wasn't here this morning, but as we fell into step behind Hector and the crew of three ride inspectors, Joe pointed back at the administration building.

"Look who's here," he said darkly.

Two suit-wearing figures stumbled out of the office building.

"Yoo-hoo! Wait for us, please!" Derek Piperato called. He was followed by Greg and a woman holding a large, professional-looking video camera. "Our videographer has just arrived!"

Hector sighed, glaring at the Piperatos. "I will say *again* that I don't feel that filming this inspection is appropriate."

The Piperatos just smiled and joined the group.

"We only quadrupled your business with the last video, Hector," Derek said with a smirk. "Maybe you'd better leave the marketing to us."

Hector grumbled something unintelligible, and we all followed him. Early-morning sunlight glinted off the polished silver sides of the ride, which looked infinitely more menacing than it had that first night we saw it. Cal stepped out from the operation booth and came down the steps to meet the inspectors. I watched as they each shook his hand, clearly remembering him from their previous inspection.

"Let me take you in," Cal said, gesturing to the ride. He opened it up, and in they went.

Joe and I didn't want to interfere with the official inspection, so we hung back while the inspectors did their work. From our vantage point just a few yards from the ride platform, we could watch the Piperato Brothers directing the videographer.

"I'm thinking of something along the lines of, 'Another one missing. Inspectors can't figure out what's going wrong. Are *you* brave enough to risk it?'" Greg said.

"That's good," Derek said, "but somewhere in there we need the line 'The Death Ride has claimed another victim.'

I'm convinced that branding this the Death Ride is responsible for at least half the response!"

"Good point," Greg agreed. "How about, 'The Death Ride has claimed another victim. Inspectors can't figure out what's wrong. The cops don't know where the victims are. Are *you* brave enough to risk . . . DUN DUN DUN . . .'"

"THE DEATH RIDE!" Derek joined in, and both Piperato brothers started laughing.

"Make sure you get lots of creepy footage—weird angles, odd lighting," Derek said casually to the videographer.

Suddenly Hector strode purposefully over to the brothers. He looked at Derek and held up a fist. "Do you actually want me to hit you?" he shouted.

Derek stumbled back, looking stunned. "Why would you hit me?" he asked. "I'm saving your amusement park!"

Hector took in a breath, like he was trying to calm himself down. "Two children are missing off this thing," he said, gesturing to G-Force. "We don't know where they are. *Do you understand that?*"

Derek looked puzzled. He shot an inquisitive look at his brother, who also seemed confused.

"Of course we do," said Greg. "And it's terrible. But we can't control that. We can only control how we respond."

"We designed a phenomenal ride," Derek added, "and now its legacy is being overshadowed by a crime or prank that we had nothing do with. We're trying to protect our own reputation here."

"Yeah," Greg agreed. "The ride wasn't designed to hurt anybody. You must know that. Whatever's going on here, it isn't our fault."

Hector sighed. "I do know that," he said. "But this is still a tragic event. Right?"

Greg and Derek looked at each other. After a moment, Derek shrugged. "It could be," he said. "Or it could be kids pulling a prank. Either way, why shouldn't we get as much publicity for our ride out of it as we can?" He nodded at the videographer. "When the inspectors are done in there, let's get some footage of the seat with the restraints cut. Okay?"

Something seemed to snap in Hector. He sprang forward and grabbed Greg by the arm. "I want you out," he said in a low, furious voice.

Derek jumped into action, pushing Hector off his brother. "What are you doing? Stop it! We're within our contractual rights!"

Hector let go of Greg and yelled, "GET OUT OF MY PARK!"

That seemed to get through to them. The Piperato Brothers scrambled around, gathering their belongings and their videographer, then scurried away from G-Force and along the path that led back to the service entrance and out of the park. Hector straightened up and watched them go, a thoughtful look in his eye.

I glanced at Joe, and together we gently approached Hector.

"Wow," I said quietly when we were just a few feet away.

Hector shook his head. "Buying this from those idiots was the worst decision I've ever made," he said in a low voice. "Worse than buying this park, even."

Before we could reply, he turned and disappeared into the ride.

Joe and I waited around while the inspectors completed their business, confirming that G-Force seemed to be in perfect working order and that there was nothing wrong with the ride itself.

The ride was just a crime scene. Not the criminal.

When the inspectors left, we stepped up onto the ride platform, waiting for a chance to get Cal alone. He puttered around for a few minutes, checking things, then locking up. Finally he strode toward the stairs—right into our path.

"Cal," Joe called, stepping out to block him. "Can we talk to you for a minute?"

Cal glanced at us, then at his watch. "Sure, boys," he said after a moment. "What can I help you with this morning?"

I gestured to G-Force. "The inspectors—have they found an alternate entrance to the ride, besides the front door?"

Cal glanced back where I was pointing. "No, they didn't find nothing like that," he said, shaking his head. "This is still a mystery, boys. I hope those kids are okay."

I leaned in. "And you don't know of another entrance to the ride?" I asked. "One that comes through the floor, maybe?"

Cal looked me in the eye. For a moment, I saw a flash of concern pass over his features, but it quickly dissipated. He shook his head. "No, sir," he said. "The only way in is through the front door. No hidden entrances, no hidden passages."

I looked at Joe. I didn't like where this was going. But I had no choice but to call Cal on his lie.

I pulled out my smartphone. "You sure about that?"

Tapping on the screen, I brought up the video I'd taken of our ride. I turned it on, and Cal watched it, looking mystified. At the 3:32 mark, I paused the video and pointed at the screen.

"See that figure?" I said. "Let me show you again."

I backed the video up so that it started just as the figure rose up through the floor.

Cal watched it, his eyes widening. He swallowed hard and took a step back.

"That looks an awful lot like you," Joe pointed out.

Cal was fidgeting nervously with his hands, folding them, unfolding them. He lifted his right index finger to his lips and bit down hard on the nail. The color was draining from his face.

"Ah, I don't know . . . ," he said, not making eye contact.

"I just . . . You know, I might remember something. . . ."

The impact came as fast and as hard as a bowling ball dropped on you from ten feet above. Suddenly I was grabbed by the back of the neck and shoved hard into G-Force's shiny silver side. Pain exploded in my head, and the edges of my vision blurred. Out of the corner of my eye, I saw Cal opening up the door of the ride. . . .

Before I understood what was happening, I was roughly shoved into the darkness. As I tried—and failed—to get up, Joe was pushed through the door too and landed in a heap beside me.

"I'm sorry, boys," Cal's voice came from somewhere above us. "I really am. . . ."

Then the door slammed shut, and everything went dark.

UNDER THEIR NOSES

NOSES

10

JOE

IT WAS PITCH-DARK INSIDE, WITHOUT EVEN A shaft of light entering from anywhere. It was like being inside a cave. Thankfully, since the ride had been up and running for the inspectors, the air-conditioning lingered, and it wasn't too hot.

"Now what?" said Frank, sighing deeply.

"I guess we know Cal's involved," I said to the deep blackness to my left, from which Frank's voice had come.

I could hear him nodding. "Involved enough to be scared," he agreed. He sighed again. "I guess we'd better try to get out of here."

"Right."

I stumbled in the dark until I hit what felt like a wall, then banged on the shiny metal side of G-Force as hard as

I could. "HELP! HELP! IS ANYONE OUT THERE?" I paused. "Is this thing soundproof? Do you remember?"

"I dunno." Frank seemed to think. "I don't remember hearing anyone screaming from inside."

I groaned. "I have a test in geometry today."

I could hear the smile in Frank's voice. "And you think 'A criminal carnie locked me inside an amusement ride' isn't an acceptable excuse?"

I started pounding the walls with my fists again. "CAL! HECTOR! DAISY! ANYONE!!"

Frank joined in. "WE'RE TRAPPED IN HERE! WE'RE INSIDE G-FORCE!"

All in all, it probably wasn't that long before Hector doubled back and found us. It felt like hours, but must have been just a few minutes before we heard a "Hello?" and the door slowly swung open. "Who's in there?"

From that point on, it was hours of explaining, telling the same story countless times to countless people.

I did end up missing my geometry test, but only because once Hector called the police, it took a long time to get everything straight. Chief Olaf came back with a whole team. Two officers were sent to Cal's apartment to look for him, and G-Force was opened up again, this time for a crew of police inspectors.

About an hour later, one of the inspectors came running out, shaking a flashlight. "We found it!"

Frank and I were sitting on a bench with Chief Olaf,

and when we looked at him pleadingly, he seemed to understand.

"All right, boys," he said under his breath. "I probably shouldn't do this, but come take a look with me."

We stood and mounted the little platform that led to the ride's door, then ducked and stepped inside. The police had brought in big floodlights, and the interior was lit up like a baseball stadium. It looked totally different from the way it did when we'd entered to go on the ride. With the bright light shining, you could see that the interior walls were cheap plastic, not metal, and that the plush purple fabric that covered the seats was not all that plush—or that clean.

The officer who'd called out, a tall man with sandy blond hair and a mustache, signaled to Chief Olaf. "It's over here," he said, pointing to an indentation in the floor that sat in the middle of the seats and was set off by a short metal railing. He reached out and grabbed a section of railing, and it came loose in his hand. A hidden gate! Then Olaf stepped down into the lowered section. Looking down, I could see that the shaggy purple carpet had been pulled up.

As we watched, the officer shone his flashlight in a small rectangle along the floor. I gasped as I realized what he was pointing out: a tiny raised lip on the floor, hidden beneath the carpet while the ride was in motion.

A trapdoor.

"There's a catch here," the officer said, pushing down with his toe on one of the short sides of the rectangle. It sprang up easily, clearly on springs, and the officer reached down to grab the raised section and swing it upward.

The trapdoor opened onto a tiny, closetlike room.

We all peered inside as the officer shone his flashlight in. The secret room was nothing more than a dark, tiny box hidden in the floor of the ride. There was nothing on the polished metal walls, nothing on the concrete floor. The officer shone his light on a tiny plastic flashlight that had been left in the corner.

The whole room was barely large enough for Frank or me to fit into, crouched down on all fours.

"So we're thinking this is where he placed them while the ride was in motion," the officer said. "It appears to be soundproof."

Chief Olaf winced, passing his hand over his face. "All right. So he sneaks in while the ride is in motion and cuts the restraints. He takes the victim and forces them down the step, opens the trapdoor, and pushes them in. How does he keep them quiet while he's doing all this?"

There was silence for a few seconds, and I cleared my throat. Chief Olaf turned to me.

"He wouldn't have to," I explained. "The ride is pretty loud, and kids are screaming the whole time. If the victim put up a fight, it would probably just blend into the background noise."

Chief Olaf grimaced and nodded. I looked into the tiny room. It was really giving me the willies to imagine Kelly and Luke trapped in there, only a flashlight to keep them company until Cal could get them out. Who knows how long they were down there? Who knows what happened to them when they were finally let out?

"So when they disappeared," Olaf said, "all the time we spent looking for them, searching a twenty-mile radius, they were right here." He sighed. "Under our noses."

I looked into the little room again and felt my stomach lurch. All at once, I realized what was happening and ran to the little door, shoving an officer or two out of the way as I went.

I got onto the platform and managed to stagger down the steps before I lost my meager breakfast on the grass just outside the ride.

Thinking about what had happened to Luke and Kelly was way worse than riding G-Force ten times in a row.

A few days later, I met Frank in the school parking lot after taking my makeup geometry test. (It turns out that teachers are pretty understanding when the cops are involved.) His expression was grim, and I could tell immediately that he was thinking about the G-Force case.

"What did you learn?" I asked.

He frowned as he pulled out and drove slowly to the parking lot exit.

"They found Cal's fingerprints all over the trapdoor," he said. "Still no sign of him, though." He pulled out of the parking lot and began the short drive home.

"No," I said, not surprised. The officers sent to find Cal when he'd run off had found an empty, ransacked apartment with no evidence of anyone being kept there. They'd been tracking Cal's activity, but nobody had used his credit cards or cell phone, and random searches set up on the roads leading out of town had turned up nothing. He'd simply disappeared.

"And I asked Chief Olaf about Cal's criminal history," Frank added. "It's just as Hector told us. Burglaries and thefts as a kid. The incident Hector mentioned at his last job isn't on his criminal history, but the police called his last employer, and that story checks out too. He did threaten a female coworker."

I was silent for a few minutes as we drove the quiet residential streets, mulling that over. So Cal had threatened a coworker. That was very different from kidnapping two teenagers off an amusement ride, for who knows what purpose. There was something about Cal that just didn't add up.

"Do you feel like we're missing a crucial part of the story?" I asked Frank.

He let out a deep sigh. "Yes," he said, sounding relieved that I felt the same way. "It's driving me crazy."

"How does Cal go from stealing cars twenty years ago to kidnapping two kids he doesn't know?" I asked. The police had tried to find connections between Cal and Kelly and Cal and Luke, but had come back with nothing. It really seemed that the two teenagers had never come in contact with Cal before they rode G-Force.

Frank was nodding. "Hector acted pretty strange when we asked him about it too. I still don't understand why he would hire Cal if he had reservations about him."

"It's like he's hiding something," I said.

We had just turned onto our street, and we were quiet as Frank pulled into the driveway, both thinking this over.

He turned off the car, still staring straight ahead.

Finally he spoke. "Just for giggles," he said, unclasping his seat belt and throwing open the door, "let's do an Internet search on Hector Rodriguez."

There was a Hector Rodriguez, apparently, who was a pretty big heartthrob on a Colombian soap opera called *La Corazón Violeta*. There was also a Hector Rodriguez based in Cushing, Maine, who sold car parts on the Internet. There was a Hector Rodriguez who'd written a very enlightening article about nesting instincts in white mice for a scientific journal in 2007.

It took us six pages of results before we got to our Hector Rodriguez.

"Hector Rodriguez, Jamaica, New York," Frank read off. "Jamaica is part of New York City, right?"

"It's part of Queens," I said, "I think."

Frank clicked on the link. It was an old article from something called the *Queens Courier*, scanned in by hand. (Clearly this article predated the newspaperzsite.) JAMAICA BOY WINS PRESTIGIOUS SCHOLARSHIP FOR CHANGING HIS WAYS was the headline.

JAMAICA—High school senior Hector Rodriguez, 18, says his future looks bright. "I have the opportunity to go to college now," he tells a reporter. "My parents are so proud. And two years ago, this wouldn't have seemed possible."

Indeed. Two years ago, it might have seemed more likely that Rodriguez would end up in prison once he reached adulthood. The teenager admits that he spent his free time prowling the streets, often engaging in criminal acts like burglaries and car theft. "I was bored," he says. "I didn't know better."

But in the last year, Rodriguez cleaned up his act and rededicated himself to his studies. He now maintains a 3.2 GPA at Bayside High School, and last week he was chosen as the recipient of the Daniel J. Elliott Scholarship Award for Previously Troubled Youth.

"We are so proud of Hector," says board member Maggie Elliott. "He's completely changed his life in a short amount of time, and he deserves the best chance he can get for a successful future."

A tiny photograph was printed alongside the article. He was decades younger and had considerably more hair, but that definitely looked like Daisy's father staring back at us.

"Huh," I said, not sure what to make of this.

"So Hector had a rap sheet too," Frank said, tapping his lip. "At one point. When he was young."

"It's weird that he neglected to mention that to us," I said. "I mean, since Cal's crimes are all from his youth too."

Frank and I looked at each other.

"Search for Cal Nevins," I suggested on a whim. "Cal Nevins of Jamaica, New York."

Frank typed all that in, and this time only one article popped up.

It was from the *New York News*. STRING OF CAR THEFTS TROUBLES JAMAICA RESIDENTS.

Frank clicked on the link, and we quickly skimmed down. The article was talking about a string of four or five car thefts that had occurred in the same neighborhood about twenty years ago—right around the time Hector got his scholarship.

The last paragraph contained an intriguing bit of information.

> Cal Nevins, 18, a local teenager, has confessed to the most recent crime, the theft of a white Chevrolet Cavalier from Bayside High School teacher Peter Winewski. Although the police admit that fingerprints collected from the car do not match Nevins's or Winewski's prints, they have accepted Nevins's confession and have sentenced him to two years in prison.

I whistled. "Two years," I said, shaking my head. "That's a long time. Especially so young."

Frank pointed at the screen. "I'm more interested in this bit here," he said. "'Fingerprints collected from the car do not match Nevins's or Winewski's.' Do you think there's a chance he didn't do it?"

I frowned. "Why would he confess if he didn't do it?"

Frank turned to me with a knowing look. "Maybe he was covering for somebody?"

"Joe!"

Daisy opened her front door looking pleased to see me, and I felt a little twist in my gut. I'd been neglecting her ever since the G-Force case kicked into high gear. I really liked her, but I have a tendency to disappear into a case . . . which is not exactly great for the love life.

Now I pasted on a smile. "Hey, Daisy. I . . . missed you. I thought we could hang out."

Daisy smiled back. "That sounds great. I'm actually making brownies. Let me stick them in the oven, and maybe we could watch a DVD."

"Perfect."

Daisy led me into the small but neat living room, where she gestured to the couch. "Seriously, I just need to put them in the pan and put the pan in the oven. Shouldn't take me five minutes. You check out our DVD collection and pick out something you like."

She walked over to a bookshelf, picked up a big book-style DVD organizer, and then walked back to hand it to me.

"Oof!" I said jokingly.

Her eyes crinkled. "We like movies in this family," she said with a chuckle. "You can rule out the second half. Those are all in Spanish."

I nodded. "Thanks for the tip."

Daisy smiled again, then gestured to the kitchen. "I'll be right back," she said, and then disappeared down the hallway.

As soon as her footsteps disappeared down the hall, I set the DVD book on the couch next to me. I'd been in Daisy's house a couple of times before. When we first started dating, she'd invited me over for a family barbecue. I'd spent just enough time inside to know that Hector's home office was the next room down the hall toward the kitchen.

Stealthily, I stood up and tiptoed to the entrance to the living room. I listened, and could hear Daisy scraping the sides of a bowl in the kitchen at the end of the hall.

I sucked in a breath and walked down the hall and into Hector's office.

Hector's home office was actually nicer than his Funspot one—possibly because Daisy's mother also used this one to do Funspot's accounting. An older desktop computer sat on a neat wooden desk, and dark wooden bookshelves, all laden with books, lined the walls.

I searched the titles on the shelves as fast as I could. On the shelves behind Hector's desk, I found what I was looking for—tall, thick hardcover tomes that could only be one thing.

Yearbooks.

I scanned the spines. Some were from Ocean City, New Jersey—those must be Daisy's mom's. But next to those I found three bright orange books with blue foiled lettering on the side: BAYSIDE HIGH SCHOOL. I selected the one from the same year as Cal's confession and pulled it out.

I quickly flipped it open and started scanning the signatures on the endpapers. *Fatima Lupo, Billy Cardigan, Jamal Parker, Deanna Vanuto.* Finally I flipped open to the senior photos and scanned the names. *McMahon, Miele, Murray, Mynowski* . . . I flipped the page.

A smiling, fresh, young Cal Nevins stared back at me. He looked utterly different from the man I'd met. More innocent. Happier.

I could hear Daisy clanging a pan around in the kitchen. She must be about to put the brownies in. I had to hurry. I flipped to the back of the yearbook and began crazily searching the signatures. *No . . . no . . . no . . .*

There it was. Two pages from the back, a full-page note. But the only part that mattered to me was the salutation.

To Hector, my best friend, my brother from another mother, I'm so proud of you. . . .

"*What* are you doing?"

You would think I'd be used to getting caught snooping by now, but I still jumped about three feet in the air, dropping the yearbook to the floor. Daisy did not sound the least bit amused. When I pulled myself together enough to turn around, I saw that she wore a hurt expression, with a crease of confusion tucked between her eyebrows.

"I'm sorry," I blurted.

"Is this for the case?" she asked, moving forward. She stepped around me to pick up the yearbook, examining the cover. "This is my father's. Do you suspect my father now?"

I shook my head. I had absolutely no idea what to say. "Not exactly. I, ah . . . I was just passing your father's study and . . . I got curious . . ."

Daisy was frowning at me. I could tell she wasn't buying any of this. "Did you really come over here to spend time with me?" she asked.

You would also think I would be a really smooth liar by now. I'm not.

"Ah . . . ah . . . I . . ."

Daisy sighed and shook her head. "I don't think this is going to work out, Joe. I like you, but . . . you never tell me what's going on. I think you'd better leave."

I found my voice then. "I'm so sorry, Daisy."

And I was. But I had to admit that somewhere along the line things got turned around: Now solving the case was more important to me than getting the girl.

We Hardys are messed up that way.

Daisy took my arm and led me to the door. "Good-bye, Joe. And obviously, you don't have to work on my dad's case anymore. I think we're fine without you."

I was out on the stoop with the door slammed in my face before I could even reply.

TRUE CONFESSIONS

11

FRANK

"S O SHE THREW YOU OUT," I SAID WITH sympathy as Joe and I dug into bowls of Aunt Trudy's homemade maple-cinnamon ice cream. It's better than Ben & Jerry's, I swear. Cure for whatever ails you.

Joe ate a spoonful and nodded. "She slammed the door in my face. Not that I can really blame her."

"It had to be kind of a shock to find you snooping in her dad's stuff," I said.

Joe sighed and nodded again. "I don't know how else I could have done it, though. She would never have let me in there. Remember how upset she was when we questioned Luke? Imagine if she knew we suspected her dad of hiding something."

I nodded sympathetically, eating my ice cream. It was true. Even though she'd hired us, Daisy had been a little touchy about us investigating her case—almost as though she wanted to do it with us.

"Maybe it's for the best," I said.

Joe poked at his ice cream. "Maybe," he said. "I have to admit, I don't think Daisy and I were meant to be. Not if she can't handle my investigating things."

I nodded, spooning up the dregs of my ice cream and wishing there was more.

"And Hector *was* hiding something," I pointed out, hoping it was okay to change the subject.

Joe nodded, looking relieved to talk about this. "Cal was his best friend. His *best friend*." He paused. "Strange how that didn't come up when we talked to him earlier."

"And strange how his own criminal history never came up—only Cal's," I added.

"He could never explain why he hired Cal even though he didn't trust him," Joe said. "It seems almost like Cal had something on him."

"Like that they were both bad kids?" I suggested. "That Hector's rap sheet was just as long as Cal's? Until he reformed."

Joe cocked an eyebrow. "Unless Hector never really reformed."

We were quiet for a few seconds, letting that sink in. I thought of the articles we'd found. Hector's not wanting

Daisy to talk to Cal. All that Hector had riding on Funspot's success, and what Cal had done to derail it.

"I think we need to talk to Hector," I said.

"Hi there, boys." Hector looked surprised, and not entirely happy, to see us standing outside his Funspot office bright and early the next morning. I was sure he'd heard about Joe and Daisy's breakup from his daughter—and also, possibly, that Joe had been snooping around in his office.

So if his friendliness had lessened a little, I guess I could understand.

"We need to talk to you," Joe said simply, without hesitating. "Is this a good place?"

Hector looked from him to me. He sighed. "As good a place as any," he said, sitting back in his chair. I noticed that he didn't invite us to sit down.

"You knew Cal as a kid," I said, wanting to cut to the point as quickly as possible.

A flicker of surprise moved across his face, quickly followed by resignation. "How did you find that out?" he asked.

"A combination of the Internet and your high school yearbooks," Joe admitted. "I'm sorry for snooping. But I had the sense you weren't being entirely honest with us."

Hector looked from us down to his desk. Suddenly his expression changed to utter despair. He put his head in his hands and groaned. "I didn't want to believe he would do this," he said miserably. "I still can't believe it!"

I glanced at Joe. Poor guy. But we still needed the whole story.

"Why don't you start at the beginning?" I asked.

Hector sighed again and ran his hands through his hair. Then he sat up in his chair and seemed to try to pull himself together. "Cal was my best friend growing up," he said. "We lived in Queens. You probably know that already."

Joe nodded. "Jamaica, right?" he asked.

"Yeah," Hector said. "There were some tough guys in our neighborhood. Gang members, petty criminals. Cal and I, we both got into some trouble when we were kids. Our mothers worked, we had a lot of free time on our hands. And we were troublemakers. We gave our parents a hard time." He sighed.

"Go on," I urged.

"We started stealing cars and breaking into places when we were teenagers," Hector said. "Younger than you two. Think middle school. It was stupid of us. We almost always got caught, and by high school we both had terrible records. It was then—when I was a junior in high school—that I realized what an awful path I was on. I had to make some changes if I was going to survive. I was going to be eighteen soon, and charged as an adult if I got into trouble again. I knew I couldn't survive in prison. I wasn't that tough."

He looked down at the desk again. "So when I was sixteen, I just stopped. I retired as a criminal. I cleaned up my act. For a year or more I studied hard, I excelled in school. I pulled up my GPA to a B. When I was a senior, I applied for a scholarship for troubled kids who'd reformed themselves—and I won it. Suddenly I was going to college!"

Joe nodded. "But then . . . ?"

Hector's face fell. "Then . . . I had a chemistry teacher at the time who was really hard to please. I was never good at being on time, and one time I was late to his class—the third time that semester, I think—he announced that he was giving me a zero on the test that day. I started doing the math in my head, and I realized I could fail the whole semester—just because of being ten minutes late. Can you imagine?"

"Yeah," I admitted. Every high school seems to have a legendarily tough teacher like the one Hector was describing. Bayport actually had several—but I'd been lucky enough to stay on their good sides so far.

Hector shook his head. "Anyway. I tried to talk to the guy, but he wouldn't listen. I was furious. I told Cal what was going on, and of course he felt terrible for me. He was almost as excited about my scholarship as I was. He'd planned to work for a couple years, save up some money, and join me at college. We talked about starting a landscaping business together."

"But," I suggested.

"But," Hector repeated, sighing. "This teacher was going to ruin my chances, or so I thought. So I suddenly had this great idea. I would steal his car to get back at him."

I raised my eyebrows. Really?

"It was stupid," Hector said quickly, seeing my expression. "Of course I realize that now. But I was angry, so angry. So I did it. After school that day, I stole the guy's car—right out of the teachers' parking lot. I was planning to keep it for a few days and then return it—just to teach the guy a lesson. But he reported it missing right away. And they found the car—parked in a vacant lot right by my house."

He shook his head and sighed again.

"It was only a matter of time until I got caught. I'd been sloppy and my fingerprints were all over the dashboard. So I told Cal what I'd done, and he didn't hesitate. 'I'll take the rap for you,' he said. I tried to tell him no, it wasn't worth it, but he insisted. He said I would have done the same for him. And he said he'd take the sentence, a couple years or whatever—and then I could pay him back. Help him get into college, or find a job. He said he knew I'd make it up to him." Hector closed his eyes and shook his head.

"So Cal was arrested," I supplied. "And sent to prison for two years."

Hector nodded. "I tried to pay him back," he said in a strained voice. "I really did. But the Cal who came out of prison wasn't the same kid who'd gone in. He was different, almost broken. He struggled with drugs, he couldn't commit to anything. I set him up in community college, and he wouldn't keep up with the classes. Finally I gave up. I cut off all ties with him."

"Wow," I said. "That must have been hard."

Hector nodded again. "It was the hardest thing I've ever done. But I saw that I wasn't helping him, I was enabling him. I hoped that if I cut him off, he'd see that he had to get his act together."

He paused. "And eventually Cal did. He started working as a carnie, traveling around the country. He got good at what he did. But I don't think he ever forgave me. I tried to reach out to him, but he always ignored my calls or letters."

"Until he showed up here," Joe said.

Hector nodded. "Until I bought Funspot, and suddenly here was Cal, applying for a job. I was thrilled, thinking we would be friends again. But Cal made clear to me that he hadn't forgiven me for abandoning him all those years ago—after all he did for me. He said he just needed the job. He was tired of traveling and wanted to be closer to home."

Joe raised his eyebrows. "So you hired him?"

"I did." Hector frowned. "But first I checked him out. I found out what I told you about his former employer— about the threat against the coworker. I told Cal my concerns, and he basically told me to hire him or I would regret it. I didn't know what he meant, but I assumed it was that he would tell everyone about the car, that it was me. And I couldn't handle Daisy knowing about that. I'd worked so hard to try to set a good example for her." He paused, then leaned forward and rubbed his eyes. He looked exhausted, I realized—like he hadn't slept in days.

"In fact," he said, "what he had planned was much worse than that. And now I feel terrible, for putting those kids in danger."

We were all quiet for a minute. I felt bad for Hector, but it was hard to get around the enormity of what had happened to Kelly and Luke as a result of whatever had gone down between Hector and Cal as kids.

"What do you think he did with them?" I asked finally. In the end, that was the only thing that mattered: getting Kelly and Luke back.

Hector looked up at me. His eyes were wet and red-rimmed. "I have no idea," he said, his voice full of despair. "I realize now that I never really knew Cal at all."

"Daddy!" Daisy's sunny voice called from the lobby, and then suddenly there she was, standing in the doorway of the office. "I went to the Coffee Stop and brought you breakfa— oh, it's you two!"

At the sight of Joe and me, Daisy's face totally changed. Her eyebrows made an angry V over her eyes, and her cheeks flushed. "Daddy, what are they still doing here? I told you they can't be trusted. They've been snooping around our house, keeping things from us—"

Hector held up his hand to stop her. "Daisy, I'm sorry," he said. "It's time I was honest with you. It's me who's been keeping things from you, not these boys. They've just stumbled onto the truth."

Daisy raised an eyebrow. "Daddy . . . what are you saying?"

Hector let out a deep sigh and then launched into an explanation of who Cal was and how they knew each other. When he got to the part about what he'd done, and how Cal had taken the blame for him and things had gone south after that, Daisy's eyes widened.

"What? Is that why you told me not to talk to him?" she asked. "Because you thought he'd tell me the truth?"

Hector nodded. "I tried so hard to be a good example for you," he said. "I didn't want you to know that I hadn't met my own standards as a kid."

Daisy's expression softened. "Dad," she said quietly. "Did you really believe I'd think any less of you? You were young and stupid. You made a mistake, that's all."

Hector's eyes watered. "Oh, sweetheart," he murmured. "You make me so proud."

Daisy shook her head. "The only thing that matters right now is finding Luke and Kelly," she said. "If what you've told me about Cal is true . . . I just don't know what he might have done with them. This is really serious."

A male voice suddenly piped up from the doorway. "You can say that again!"

SIGHTINGS 12

JOE

DEREK PIPERATO STOOD IN THE DOORway, red-faced and furious-looking.

His brother Greg ran up behind him. "We got your message," he said, as the two of them strode into the office toward Hector. "Frankly, I'm stunned. With the amount of publicity G-Force has gotten this fleabag amusement park! The only problem with the ride right now is that it *isn't running*. If you would just open back up, you'd be rolling in money!"

Hector stood up. "Your attraction has been involved in the kidnapping of two children, and frankly, I've been horrified by your reactions to the whole proceeding. I want that thing out of my park. I want you to tear it down. Take it to Wonder World; I don't care."

Derek shook his head, too upset to speak, while Greg looked at his brother and then turned back to Hector, making a big show of looking composed.

"We've been over this," he said. "We were not involved in the creation of the secret room. There was space there, yes, but the hidden trapdoor was not part of the original design. It was your ride operator who must have altered the ride—to suit his ulterior motives."

Derek suddenly leaned forward and grabbed Greg's seersucker jacket. "Ulterior motives!" he cried. "That's perfect for the next trailer." He spoke in a deep, horror-movie voice. *"He had ulterior motives . . ."*

"ENOUGH!" Hector shouted, standing up and pointing his finger at the two brothers. "You'll be hearing from my lawyers, but our association is over. G-Force is done at Funspot."

Suddenly Frank checked his watch. "Oh, wow," he said, holding it up to me. "Look at the time. We've got about five minutes to get to school."

Daisy groaned. "That means I'm going to be late too." She glared at us. "If you two hadn't been here, I'd be at school by now."

Hector sighed. "I'm sorry, Daisy—I didn't realize how late it was. But now I have this to deal with." He gestured at the red-faced Piperato Brothers. "I'm sorry, but I can't drive you to school."

Daisy turned to us and scowled.

"It's okay," Frank said. "We're headed in that direction. Can we give you a ride?"

Was he kidding? I glared at him. Frank shrugged back at me innocently.

Daisy huffed. "I guess I don't have a choice," she said, turning from me to the Piperato Brothers to her father. She put the bag from the Coffee Stop on her father's desk and hoisted her backpack higher on her shoulder. "Bye, Daddy. I'll come by later."

She strutted out the door, and Frank turned to follow her. "Thank you for the information, Hector. Will you tell the police?

Hector sighed and nodded. "Of course."

I had little choice but to follow my brother. The three of us walked out of the administration building and out to the parking lot in awkward silence.

Nobody spoke until we were in the car—I drove, because I needed something to focus on—and pulling out onto the main road.

"Did you know that it's a myth that toilets flush in the opposite direction in the southern hemisphere?" Frank piped up suddenly.

Daisy shot him a withering look. "Are you kidding me?"

"It's true," Frank said, nodding. "A toilet flushes in whatever direction you shoot the water. It's simple physics."

I tried to focus on the drive as Frank went on to try to interest Daisy in static electricity, digestion, and whale songs.

Nothing seemed to take, and soon Daisy was glaring out the window.

We were driving down the "main drag" of town—a commercial strip filled with mini malls, fast-food chains, and run-down motels. There were a bunch of stoplights, and I was cursing our timing as we got stopped at a third light. We were going to be late for sure. I glanced out the window, trying to remember what we were doing in first-period Spanish, when suddenly a slight figure walking into a dumpy convenience store caught my eye.

"Wait a minute," I said out loud, pointing. "Frank—do you see that?"

Frank turned. The figure was wearing a baseball cap and dark glasses, but the swagger was unmistakable. "Oh, wow," he said, leaning up in his seat to see better. "That's Luke!"

Daisy startled and turned around. "Are you crazy?" she demanded.

But I was already throwing the car into reverse so I could pull across three lanes of traffic and into the store parking lot.

Daisy screamed, "WHAT ARE YOU DOING? We're already late! There's no way that's him!"

But as we barreled into the parking lot, the figure turned around, spotted us, and took off running.

REVELATIONS 13

FRANK

"GET HIM!" I SHOUTED.

Joe slammed the car into park and threw the door open, forgetting for a second that he had a seat belt on. As he snapped back into his seat, I disentangled myself and sprinted out of the car after the guy. Soon I could hear Joe right behind me.

Luke was running out of the parking lot, behind the convenience store. As we drew closer he ran up to the wire fence separating the parking lot from the lot of the motel next door. He artfully inserted his foot into one of the links, launched himself up, and jumped the fence. I ran after him, scrambling up and over the fence and jumping down onto the broken asphalt with a *thud* that rattled my leg bones.

He was taking off around the nearest motel building, a

long, squat, one-story structure that looked like it had seen better days. I rocketed after him as I heard Joe climbing the fence behind me.

When I got to the front of the building, Luke was running across the parking lot, around the tiny fenced-in swimming pool, and over to the next lot, which housed a pizza joint. This lot, however, was separated from the motel by a tall plastic fence that looked impossible to climb—or jump. He stopped, looked at it for a second, and then looked back at me, seeing that I was just a few yards away.

"Give up, Luke!" I yelled. "Tell us the truth about what happened to you!"

He watched me. His dark glasses hid much of his expression, but he seemed to be considering my words. I moved closer.

Then, when I was almost close enough to touch him, he suddenly sprang back into motion, darting away from me and across the lot in the other direction—toward the street.

"Nooooo!" yelled Joe from behind me. The light had just changed, and traffic was moving by at a rapid pace.

But Luke didn't listen. He scrambled out into traffic, cars screeching to a halt and loudly honking their horns as they tried to avoid him. He reached the median, missing a pickup truck by just inches, and hopped over the narrow metal divider.

Joe ran up next to me. "Are we going to lose him?" he asked.

It was a rhetorical question, I knew. We couldn't let Luke get away after everything we'd learned. Either he was being held by Cal and had escaped by now, or there was another, more complicated, reason for his appearance.

"Let's go," I said simply, and ran toward the street.

I tried to bob and weave through the cars, but the drivers still didn't like that much. Traffic was moving around forty miles an hour, and suddenly I was trapped in a real-life game of Frogger. (That's an old arcade game. I like vintage arcade games.)

A red sports car in the second lane screeched to a halt just inches from my feet. The driver, a pretty blond lady, was so mad that she reached out the open window and threw her iced coffee at me.

Luckily, I *was* able to avoid that.

I scrambled over the median. I could hear the cars honking in protest as Joe followed me. On the other side of the road traffic was lighter, and I was able to cross without causing too much of a problem.

Luke was running around an old candy store and into the lot of another run-down motel.

He must have thought he'd lost us, because he slowed a little as he ran into the motel parking lot. He paused and looked around, and I grabbed Joe and ducked down behind a minivan in the candy store parking lot to watch. What was he doing?

When he was satisfied that Joe and I were gone, Luke casually strolled up to a motel room on the right—this motel was made up of ramshackle buildings whose rooms all faced the parking lot—and knocked. The door opened, and he disappeared inside.

"Room thirty-four," Joe observed, straightening up beside me.

"Room thirty-four," I echoed. "Do we call the police?"

Joe nodded. "Oh yeah," he said. "I'm not walking into this one alone."

He pulled his cell phone out of his pocket and hit the speed dial for the Bayport PD.

"OPEN UP! POLICE!"

Chief Olaf and an officer were crouched outside the door to room 34, guns cocked. They hammered on the door, and for a long time nothing happened. You could hear muffled voices inside, like the inhabitants were debating what to do. Just as Olaf gave the officer a meaningful glance, like they should break the door down, we could hear the scrabble of the cheap chain lock against the wooden door, and then the door opened inward.

Olaf nearly lost his balance, but he recovered quickly.

Luke was standing at the door. He stepped back, allowing the police to enter. Joe and I followed.

Inside, on one of the sunken double beds, sat Kelly, sipping a McDonald's shake.

"What's going on here?" The chief demanded, looking from one missing kid to the other.

Luke looked sheepish. He glanced behind Olaf to Frank and me, and his eyes narrowed in a glare. Then he turned back to the policemen, and his expression cleared.

"It was a hoax," he said simply.

Over the next couple of hours at the Bayport police station, Luke and Kelly told us the whole sordid tale.

"The idea was to get more publicity for G-Force, and for Funspot," he explained. "But I don't think Hector knew anything about it."

"I'm sure he didn't," said Daisy. Once the police had Luke and Kelly loaded into their squad car, Joe and I had gone back to the car to find a very teed-off Daisy. Luckily for us, she'd softened when we told her what happened.

"Tell us how this all started," Chief Olaf said.

Luke sighed and gestured to Kelly that she should start.

"A few weeks before the opening, I got an e-mail," she said. "It was from an address I'd never seen before, but the sender said he knew me and thought I might like an opportunity to help start an Internet sensation, for a lot of money."

"An Internet sensation?" Olaf repeated, like the words tasted sour.

Kelly nodded. "It was a brand-new marketing idea, was how they described it. All I had to do was pretend to disappear on the ride, and hide for a few weeks in a motel until the search died down. I'd get free meals, a few weeks off school, and a thousand dollars for my trouble."

Chief Olaf's eyes softened. "That must have seemed like a lot of money to a girl your age."

Kelly frowned at him. "It's not just that. My mom works three jobs already. I'm too young to work. I thought maybe this was a way to help out my family."

"Except that they'd go crazy with panic thinking you were missing for weeks," Olaf pointed out.

Kelly nodded, looking a little ashamed. "I know. I felt terrible about that. But I told myself it would all be okay when I came home, safe and sound. They'd be so relieved—plus we'd have the money."

"So you said yes," I said.

Kelly nodded. "Right. I e-mailed back and said I'd do it."

"How did you know what to do—what would happen when you 'disappeared'?" Olaf asked.

Kelly reached into her pocket and pulled out a folded printout. "I got this back," she replied.

The chief took the printout and unfolded it. I could read over his shoulder. There was a diagram of the inside of G-Force, like a map, with the seats numbered. *Sit in seat #6,* it said clearly. *Someone will help you out during the ride. Follow him and don't ask any questions.*

Olaf pointed to the e-mail address at the top of the page. *D@piperatobros.com,* it read. "Anyone familiar with that e-mail?"

"Derek Piperato," Joe and I said in unison.

Olaf turned to Kelly. "Does that sound familiar?"

She shrugged. "I don't know. I never met him," she said. "A guy named Cal got me out of the seat and told me what to do. When I was able to leave the ride that night, he took me to this motel. He was bringing us food and making sure we were okay, but he stopped a week or so ago." He gestured to Luke. "Luke's been taking care of us since then."

Luke nodded. "It's a good thing I had some money in my pocket."

He described a similar experience: the e-mail, the offer of a thousand dollars. He didn't mention needing to help his family—he wanted the money to put toward a new car. Like Kelly, he told himself that the pain he caused his family would be eliminated when he came home. And he produced an identical e-mail—from D@piperatobros.com.

"I can't believe this," Daisy muttered, shaking her head. "I can't believe it! Dad never would have gone into business with these guys if he knew they had this in them."

Chief Olaf looked at his officers. "We'd better get these Piperato Brothers in here," he said.

About half an hour later, Derek and Greg Piperato were dragged in, struggling and complaining.

"This is an outrage!" Derek cried. His handlebar mustache was all out of whack. "A travesty of justice! With what are we being charged?"

"Oh, take your pick," Olaf said, strolling out of the interrogation room to greet them. "Kidnapping, fraud, endangerment of a minor? Shall I go on?"

Greg Piperato looked indignant. "What are you talking about? What is the meaning of all this?"

The chief strolled over to the brothers with the printout Kelly had given him. "Does this look familiar?" He held it up in front of Greg's face.

I could see Greg's eyes moving back and forth as he struggled to take it all in.

"'Get out of the ride'?" he asked. "'You will be handsomely rewarded'? What does all this mean?"

"It means," Olaf said with a smile, "you didn't get away with it. And your little stunt backfired, because G-Force is dead in this town!"

G-FORCED AGAIN

14

JOE

I T'S GOING TO BE THE END OF THE SEASON SOON," Frank said, popping a piece of cotton candy in his mouth as we walked down the main drag of Funspot toward G-Force. "I guess this place will be dark until next season."

"That gives them plenty of time to tear down this ride," I agreed. "I'm sure Hector will be relieved about that."

"I'm sure you're right," Frank said. "Although the park has been pretty busy lately—no doubt all the publicity the hoax got."

For the last week straight the news had been obsessively covering the "G-Force hoax," featuring interviews with Luke, Kelly, Hector—even Derek and Greg Piperato, vigorously insisting that they were innocent in their bright orange jailhouse jumpsuits.

"I have to admit," I said, "I'm kind of looking forward to the last ride."

Tonight was G-Force's final hurrah. The Piperatos had been charged, Luke and Kelly were back with their (non-plussed, but relieved) families, and the attraction was going to be torn down starting tomorrow. But since nothing had ever been found to be wrong with the ride itself, Hector had agreed to open it for one last night. After that, surely, G-Force would just be one more strange appendix in amusement park history.

"It's a great little ride," Frank agreed, finishing up his cotton candy and tossing the paper cone in the trash. "Kidnapping, greed, and unnecessary drama notwithstanding."

We stepped around the food stands and found ourselves staring at G-Force—which was still pretty impressive, with its polished chrome sides gleaming in the late-afternoon sun. A huge line was already snaking around the clearing, excited kids and teenagers chatting eagerly about their last chance to go on the Death Ride. (Despite Hector's best efforts, the nickname had stuck.)

"This is where I wish you'd worked it out with Daisy," Frank said with a sigh.

"I know," I agreed. "I kind of wish we'd worked it out too. I miss her."

"I miss her connections," Frank added.

Suddenly I saw a familiar mane of dark hair moving toward me—and a familiar pink-lipsticked smile.

"Hi, Hardys."

Daisy was approaching, flanked by Penelope and Luke. I'd heard from Jamie that Daisy and Luke had maybe started seeing each other again; the whole scandal had brought them closer.

Which was hard to believe. Not that I'm bitter or anything.

"Hi, Daisy," I said. If our fledgling romance hadn't been saved when we solved the case, at least Daisy and I had been friendly again lately. That was a relief.

Daisy nodded. "You boys brave enough to risk the "Death Ride" again?" she asked, gesturing to the line.

"What can I say?" I asked. "We've been through so much together."

"And it *is* a great ride," Frank added.

Daisy glanced at him. "It's hard for me to forgive the Piperatos for what they did, but I guess you're right," she said, looking thoughtful. She turned back to me. "Want to ride it? With us?"

Frank jumped a little. I shot him a *Cool it* look. "You mean skip the line?" I asked.

Daisy smiled again, and her expression softened. "It's probably the least I can do, under the circumstances," she said gently.

I smiled back. "Well, we'll take you up on your offer then."

Daisy looked pleased. Penelope and Luke looked a little disappointed, but whatever. "Come with me," Daisy said.

We followed her across the clearing and up to the little platform where you boarded the ride. A new, dark-bearded operator was waiting there, wearing a name tag that said JAKE. Cal had never been found by the police—he still hadn't used his phone or credit card—and Hector believed that he would never come back. He was probably too ashamed that he'd taken the Piperato Brothers' money to do something he knew Hector wouldn't like. Hector said he would always miss his old friend, but he believed he was really and truly gone now.

Daisy smiled at Jake, and he quickly opened the gate to let us up. Then he led us to G-Force's door and let us inside. We chose seats—I didn't bother trying to sit next to Daisy this time—and Jake strapped us in. As we waited for him to let in the rest of the riders, I couldn't help staring into the little indentation where I knew the secret compartment lay. The trapdoor had been covered back up with the carpet, but I knew it was there.

After a few minutes the door opened up again and a bunch of rowdy kids entered and chose seats. I let my mind wander, trying not to listen to Daisy and Luke's chat or Frank trying to "break down" the physical properties of the ride for the thousandth time. Soon Jake backed out of the door and closed it behind him. The riders all erupted into spontaneous applause, eager to experience G-Force for one last, precious time.

The lights darkened. I instinctively grabbed onto my restraint bar as the opening chords of "Beautiful" started up and the ride began spinning. Soon images were flashing in the middle of the ride, and I felt myself being taken away. *That's what a good amusement park ride does for you,* I thought as we spun up and over and around again. *It takes you to another place—just for a few minutes.*

Too soon, the images slowed and the ride resumed its starting position. The music finished up, and the riders all applauded again. The seats locked into place. The lights came up.

"I'm going to miss it," I admitted to Frank, before a scream split the air.

"AUUUUUGGGGGGGGGHHHHHHHHHHHH!"

It was Penelope. I looked over at her, and my stomach clenched.

"It's Daisy!" she cried. *"She's missing! She's gone!"*

Oh no, I thought. *Could this really be happening all over again?*